Brown Face, Big Master

CARIBBEAN CLASSICS

Series Editor: John Gilmore

Titles already published:

Caribbean Classics

Brown Face, Big Master

Joyce Gladwell

Edited and with a new Introduction
by Sandra Courtman

MACMILLAN
CARIBBEAN

Macmillan Education
Between Towns Road, Oxford OX4 3PP
A division of Macmillan Publishers Limited
Companies and representatives throughout the world

www.macmillan-caribbean.com

ISBN 0 333 97430 1

Designed by Bob Elliott
Typeset by EXPO Holdings, Malaysia
Cover design by Gary Fielder, AC Design
Cover photograph by Amador Packer

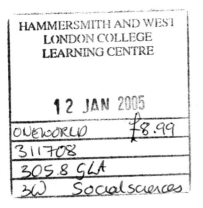

Printed and bound in Malaysia

2007 2006 2005 2004 2003
10 9 8 7 6 5 4 3 2 1

311708

CONTENTS

SERIES EDITOR'S PREFACE

Literatures often develop by drawing on their predecessors, translating, adapting, re-interpreting, and sometimes surpassing the authors from whom they take their inspiration. We can think of Shakespeare's plundering of Holinshed's *Chronicles*, James Grainger's reworking of Virgil and other writers in his eighteenth-century 'West-India georgic', *The Sugar-Cane: A Poem*, or the way in which Jean Rhys responds to Charlotte Brontë's *Jane Eyre* in *Wide Sargasso Sea*. Sometimes, however, there seems to be an entirely new beginning, because what has gone before is either unknown or actively rejected. Brought up, like Joyce Gladwell, on a literary diet of Shakespeare, Dickens, Wordsworth, Keats, Shelley and Latin unseens, many of the writers of the 1950s and 1960s who within the Anglophone Caribbean and its diaspora worked towards the creation of a 'West Indian literature,' which would reflect their own concerns and those of the people from whom they came, felt that something new and different was exactly what was required. The title of the political, literary and cultural periodical, *New World Quarterly*, established in 1963 in what was still British Guiana, represented an aspiration as well as a geographical statement.

The West Indian literature of the 1950s and 1960s in many ways was indeed new and different. For the first time a substantial body of fiction and poetry was being created which not only had at its centre the lives of the Afro-Caribbean and Indo-Caribbean working classes of the British colonies of the region as they moved towards Independence, but which was written by authors whose own roots were among such lives and who could turn the speech of street and field and yard and tenantry into a richly expressive literary vehicle. The difference gave the new literature a considerable success in the European and North American markets which enabled writers to make a living and continue to develop their craft. Growing international recognition eventually led to the award of the Nobel Prize in Literature to Derek Walcott (1992) and V. S. Naipaul (2001). By the beginning of the twenty-first century, many of us have taken to thinking, not so much of 'West Indian literature,' as of 'the literature of the Anglophone Caribbean,' recognising the growing awareness, among both writers and readers of the region, of Caribbean literatures in different languages, and the growing importance of reciprocal influences among them. The West Indian literature of the past has also done much to inspire the development of new literatures in its turn, in particular, Black British Literature and the literatures of the Caribbean diasporas in Canada and the United States of America.

However, even the new West Indian literature of the 1950s and 1960s drew – inevitably – not only on the lives and speech of Caribbean people, but on literary influences. Reading is one of the main ways in which writers learn to write, and what the West Indian writers of the period read was shaped by their colonial education. It is hardly surprising that the poetry of Kamau Brathwaite's evocations of the pains and triumphs of black peoples' lives in Africa and the Caribbean should have been influenced by T. S. Eliot as well as by jazz, or that V. S. Naipaul's exploration of the universal splendours and miseries of human destiny unfolding themselves in a very specific time and place in *A House for Mr. Biswas* should owe more than a little to the great European novelists of the nineteenth century. What difference might it have made if the new West Indian writers had been aware of earlier work written in the Caribbean in the eighteenth and nineteenth centuries? Nearly all of this was produced by writers from whom they were separated by race and class – but this could equally be said of the authors of the conventional literary canon. Brathwaite has written in his *Barabajan Poems* (1994) of the feeling he experienced on discovering that the earlier Barbadian poet, Matthew Chapman (1796–1865), had written about the 'May Dust' (a fall of volcanic ash on Barbados from an eruption in the neighbouring island of St. Vincent, long remembered in Barbadian folklore), the feeling that both of them had been 'writing the same poem' – but this was after Brathwaite had written his own May Dust poem. This is no more than a tantalising glimpse of what might have been, for the surprisingly large number of poets and novelists writing in or about the Anglophone Caribbean in the period from the late seventeenth to the late nineteenth century have generally survived only in a very few copies dispersed in institutional libraries or private collections. They were read by very few in the course of the twentieth century, and it is only in recent years that this early literature has begun to be re-explored by scholars and reprinted for the benefit of a wider readership.

The Macmillan Caribbean Classics series aims to make available once more works of Caribbean literature which have been neglected and forgotten, in the belief that – apart from their interest as documents of sociocultural history – they can still appeal to the modern reader. Previous titles in the series have been nineteenth-century novels; *Brown Face, Big Master* is the first work by a living writer to be included, and the first work of autobiography. However, Joyce Gladwell's memoir fits the series in other ways: it is a fascinating, and perhaps unique, work which after its initial success disappeared from our literary awareness for thirty years. Like other literatures, West Indian literature has its canon and, as is the case with other literatures, the reasons why some texts continue to be read and studied, while others vanish from the curriculum and from publishers' lists, can be somewhat mysterious. Not a single title by Edgar Mittelholzer or John Hearne, both once among the most successful of Caribbean writers, is currently in print. The complex reasons why *Brown Face, Big Master* successfully sold a substantial print-run and was then allowed to drop out of sight are explored in the erudite introduction to the present edition by Sandra Courtman, a leading British scholar of Caribbean literature.

As Courtman points out, however, Gladwell's book is of much greater interest than a simple case study in the politics of canon-formation. When asked about 'West Indian literature' of the 1950s and 1960s, most readers – inside the Caribbean as well as outside the region – are likely to think first of the (predominantly male) working-class emigrant/immigrant experience so memorably explored in Sam Selvon's *The Lonely Londoners* (1956) or the (again, predominantly male) novel of growing up in a colonial society whose classic representative is George Lamming's *In the Castle of My Skin* (1953). Female-authored narratives which explore somewhat different aspects of Caribbean experience, such as Merle Hodge's *Crick Crack, Monkey* (1970) or Jamaica Kincaid's *Annie John* (1985), come somewhat later. Yet the Caribbean experience which Joyce Gladwell writes about in *Brown Face, Big Master* is different again. She writes about growing up in Jamaica in the 1940s, and about being a West Indian in London in the 1950s, but it is the comparatively privileged world of the educated 'coloured' middle-class and, later, of the student rather than the working-class immigrant. It would be hard to imagine Selvon's Lonely Londoners being invited (as Gladwell's sister was) to a Buckingham Palace garden party or to take tea with the Bishop of London. Yet the framework of colonialism remains the same: the assumptions about the inferiority of 'the Negro' enshrined in the *Encyclopædia Britannica* in the library of her Jamaican boarding school, or the horror with which her intended husband's family greet the prospect of a mixed marriage.

As a spiritual autobiography, *Brown Face, Big Master* is probably unique. Religion plays an enormous part in the history and present-day life of the Caribbean, and it can certainly be found in the region's literature. A work like Austin Clarke's novelised memoir *Growing up stupid under the Union Jack* (1980) is as full of the externals of the Christian faith as it is of the Latin which played as large a part in colonial education in Barbados as it did in Jamaica – choir practices in the Anglican Cathedral and services in the Church of the Nazarene which his mother preferred. But the reader gets no sense of what it meant, in a spiritual rather than a sociological sense, to the author who maintains a detached, ironic tone even when describing how he was 'saved' in the Church of the Nazarene when 'Sister Christopher seduced me to the altar' – an experience which, presumably, had no lasting effect. There are earlier accounts written by committed Christians, such as the conversion narrative which Elizabeth Hart wrote in Antigua in 1804 (printed in Moira Ferguson, ed., *The Hart Sisters: Early African Caribbean Writers, Evangelicals, and Radicals*, 1993) or the better known *History of Mary Prince, A West Indian Slave* (1831). However, these are brief and sometimes pose special problems of interpretation (such as the question of how far Mary Prince's narrative was rewritten by her white, male editor). A prolonged and diligent searching of the archives of missionary societies and the religious press of the nineteenth century might well produce other examples, but none of these would appear to have had any direct influence on Joyce Gladwell. Written from the heart, *Brown Face, Big Master* is an account of one soul's search for the God who 'hath made of one blood all nations of men,' an account which has moved many readers in many different parts of the world. In publishing this edition, we hope that it will do so again.

John Gilmore
Centre for Caribbean Studies
and
Centre for Translation and Comparative Cultural Studies
University of Warwick

AUTHOR'S ACKNOWLEDGEMENTS

This second edition of *Brown Face, Big Master* has come about entirely due to the persistent efforts of Sandra Courtman, and for this I am gratefully indebted to you, Sandra.

To my acknowledgements in the first edition, I would like to add my gratitude to Mervyn Morris, Senior Lecturer in Classics at the University of the West Indies. He reviewed and commented in detail on the first manuscript, and encouraged me to publish it.

Joyce Gladwell

A *Rare and Fine Portrait of a West Indian Writer as a Young Woman in England*

An angel may be a fine teacher, but the world needs a witness[1]

When I wrote the title for this essay, it was meant simply to convey something of the content of Joyce Gladwell's autobiography to a readership who were unlikely to know of *Brown Face, Big Master*. I was also preoccupied with a book that I was teaching at that time, James Joyce's *A Portrait of an Artist as a Young Man*, and its celebrated depiction of the Irish experience of cultural colonisation.[2] I now see that the title of my essay problematises some key features of Gladwell's work, including her comparative obscurity which is now addressed by Macmillan's re-issue of *Brown Face, Big Master* as a Caribbean Classic.

This book undoubtedly constitutes 'a find' because for a Jamaican woman to publish a full length autobiography in 1969 was very rare indeed. It is also rare in its quality; Gladwell provides a very fine portrait of her early life in Jamaica and of her transfer to England. The book is unusual in that she depicts her life as a colonial student at London University in a period where we are more accustomed to reading about the hustling of the male economic migrant. She also gives us an insight into her remarkable spirit, both as a creative and resourceful black woman, and as a devout Christian struggling to maintain faith. Gladwell's text defies all the usual expectations of this period of Caribbean literary history and signals the extraordinary character that was necessary to produce this book and the not so extraordinary circumstances that have led to its occlusion.

'The West Indies' is Columbus's misnomer for the region which nationalism has since reclaimed as 'The Caribbean'.[3] My use of the term 'West Indian' in the title marks Gladwell's achievements historically since she is writing about the period just before Jamaica's independence in 1962. She was writing *Brown Face, Big Master* in 1963 on the very cusp of nationalist movements which transformed the British colonies into the modern world. For several reasons, the period from 1956 onwards is often claimed as a watershed in terms of cultural challenge. We should note that young Gladwell was writing at roughly the same time as Frantz Fanon, George Lamming and Sam Selvon and that she came to a British university (in 1953) as Stuart Hall, Kenneth Ramchand and other West Indian intellectuals did. In a way, Gladwell is both outside of, and part of that lost generation whose identity quests were highly politicised. We are talking about a generation who erased pre-war notions of a cultural consensus and founded a different society; even in the colonial outpost of a 1940s Jamaican boarding school, the book reveals important moves towards Black Nationalism. She is part of a generation whose intellectual enquiry would prefigure the central concerns of postcolonial theory. When we recover a text like *Brown Face, Big Master*, we also need to recover and reconstruct its socio-historical and cultural context. By definition 'lost writing', like *Brown Face, Big Master*, is unresearched, untheorised, and lies outside the discussions of an established body of criticism and cultural history. Gladwell's reemergence into the public domain should intervene in this silence; I hope that my essay can initiate the type of dialogue that will rescue *Brown Face, Big Master* from the void and give it the critical attention that it warrants.

Given that Gladwell's work appeared originally in 1969, it should raise some important questions. Caribbean literary histories of the 1960s suggest that West Indian women writers are simply non-existent (excepting the white Creole Jean Rhys). To find Gladwell writing against the grain, anticipating the rise of feminism, is unusual. In a now familiar argument, Marjorie Thorpe iterates the concerns of feminist critics and historians 'to reconstruct female experience previously hidden or overlooked'.[4] Women writers in the 1960s and 1970s were working against a West Indian male cultural hegemony which was fiercely protective of its new found cultural territory. For over thirty years, this book has been awaiting its opportunity to disrupt a popular assumption that West Indian women's experience, rich and diverse in its explication, was never published during the post-war creative boom that saw so many West Indian male writers publishing their first novels. Many women writers had to store their manuscripts until the women's presses (such as Virago and the Women's Press) and the black and small presses (such as New Beacon, Bogle L'Ouverture, Peepal Tree) legitimised their voices and gave them a public space for the first time.

Given its achievements, we might expect Gladwell's groundbreaking text to have a place in the Caribbean canon. Below I discuss how a canon that continues to privilege the novel will continue to overlook many early women writers. To scholars interested in literary history, this is a period of enormous growth in the development of the Caribbean novel, but if we look to accounts of that growth we find women's expression is largely absent. As a starting point, it might be useful to briefly sketch Gladwell's achievements into a wider context of the recuperative history of Caribbean women's writing.

Women Writers and the 'Lost Years'

If you ask a room full of literary critics to name a woman writer from the Caribbean, the majority will name Jean Rhys as arguably the most controversial and best known woman writer from the region. Rhys is often thought of as a writer from the 1960s, but much of her work was actually written in the 1930s and recovered too late for her to feel the benefit. She was, by the time it was critically acclaimed, in her seventies, alcoholic and debilitated from years of trying to write with '*No* privacy, *No* cash, *No* security, *No* resilience, *No* youth, *No* desk to write on, *No* table even, *No* one who understands.'[5] Her 'discovery', alive if not well, led to the signing of an historic publishing contract with André Deutsch for a novel that had existed in draft form for at least twenty years.[6]

Ironically, given Rhys's 'rediscovery' in the publishing boom of the 1960s and the classic status now attributed to that novel – *Wide Sargasso Sea* – this is a decade of 'lost years' for West Indian women writers more generally. Why add to the ongoing critical debate on Rhys's *Wide Sargasso Sea* when there were likely to be other equally interesting 'lost' writers from the Caribbean? This is how I came to search for and find, in 1995, Gladwell's 'lost' text *Brown Face, Big Master*. I knew that women were writing during the 1940s, 1950s and 1960s for newspapers, journals and literary magazines in the regions of the Caribbean.[7] What is striking about Rhys and Gladwell is that they were writing, albeit very differently, in response to exile and the metropolis, just as their male counterparts were.

We know that finding outlets and audiences for published writing was difficult in the colonial West Indies. This is why Selvon, Lamming and Naipaul had to travel to England to become published and recognised as writers. Rhys's generation of women were also extensive travellers to Europe and yet there appears to be very little British published material by West Indian women. When women are missing from the picture, it is bound to bury a set of complex historical conditions that have affected women's expression. There is an apparent void in West Indian women's writing which stretches between the early autobiographies of Mary Prince (1831) and Mary Seacole (1857) to Sylvia Wynter's novel, *The Hills of Hebron*, published in 1962.[8] Furthermore, it would appear that very little writing was published in the 1960s and 1970s which might have begun to fill this void. As a researcher confronted with an obvious gap in women's expression, I seek answers to certain questions: why is it that so many West Indian women only began to be known as 'writers' in the 1980s? What historical conditions would encourage or prevent women from writing? Who was writing, what were they writing about and in what forms? Who had access to publishing and what type of publishing was available to them? What happened to their writing and how might this have affected their subsequent careers? What do we learn from their writing about general developments in Caribbean and Black-British attempts to find a voice in the literary media? Writing like Gladwell's forms part of the recovery of that hidden history in that it tells us much about their development, what choices of expression they made, and why. Post-war accounts of Caribbean history emphasise the importance of *transition* – from colonial to independent, from patriarchal to feminist, from migrant to Black-British – and these transitions are crucial to the history of women's literary expression. Gladwell's text helps us to trace women's struggles to find forms and voices – themselves largely lost within those transitions – which were to play an important part in freeing up a new postcolonial literary space for the next generation of Caribbean women writers. We need to recover texts like Gladwell's because we need to understand her struggles in the context of a history of race, gender and class determinants.

Undoubtedly, one of the reasons for an absence of early women writers in accounts of the literary history of the Caribbean has been the tendency to privilege the novel over other forms of expression. It could be argued that the field of West Indian literature was created in 1970, when Kenneth Ramchand published his ground-breaking work of scholarship, *The West Indian Novel and its Background*. Ramchand's work surveyed the historical and aesthetic development of the West Indian novel and, in doing so, he continued to valorise an exclusive cultural form that would be inappropriate for the majority of West Indian women. But even those women who had published novels were largely written out of Ramchand's 1970 year-by-year Appendix; his list of 169 novels published between 1903 and 1967 contained just five entries for women.[9] My research reveals a tentative (though much improved) figure of thirty-two published novels from 1948 to 1979. Even so, it is this paucity of novels by West Indian women that maintains their exclusion from literary histories such as Ramchand's and which continues to be promoted in later surveys.

By the end of the twentieth century, Maya Jaggi celebrates a new and flourishing generation of Black-British novelists. Out of the five pictured in her piece for *The Guardian*, four are female. It is clear that much has been achieved by these 'New Brits on the Block'. She acknowledges the young novelists' debt to Sam Selvon, George Lamming and Kamau Brathwaite, as the quintessential 'West Indian on the Final Passage' writers. Jaggi doesn't find any female role models but reinforces West Indian male writers' achievements during the 1950s and early 1960s.[10] Of these novels of 40 years ago that were published by women, those generally known and cited are by white West Indians such as Rhys, Phyllis Shand Allfrey and Ada Quayle.

To date, feminist literary scholarship on the Caribbean rarely helps us to understand why black women writers are absent from the period in which Gladwell was writing her autobiography. Pioneering work on Caribbean women's writing, notably Carole Boyce Davies and Elaine Fido Savory, *Out of the KUMBLA*; Evelyn O'Callaghan, *Woman Version: Theoretical Approaches to West Indian Fiction by Women*; Selwyn R. Cudjoe, ed., *Caribbean Women Writers: Essays From the First International Conference*; and Mary Conde and Thorunn Lonsdale, *Caribbean Women Writers: Fiction in English*, focuses on work published since the 1980s or on a smattering of white West Indians of a generation earlier, such as Rhys.[11]

As if to highlight this absence, in 1980, C.L.R. James gave an interview to Daryl Dance. James, the author of one of the earliest known black Caribbean novels, *Minty Alley* (1936), admires the achievements of African-American writers, Walker and Morrison. Dance prompts him to comment on equivalent women writers from the Caribbean. He replies by paying tribute to Sylvia Wynter as an exceptional 'writer of history and a critic of politics' (ignoring her 1962 novel). But his final comment is dismissive because he and George Lamming are looking for a novelist to award their recognition:

> James: *We* have not produced the women writers as yet. George Lamming tells me that he is waiting for the woman in the Caribbean to write a novel which will state the position of the Caribbean. Well, he is waiting for her. I am waiting for her too.[12]

This is perhaps not surprising since James and Lamming were very much preoccupied, in their own work, with how to write a novel that would account for the lives of the black majority population of the Caribbean. They grappled with the problem of representation in a scribal form that was of little value to the poor black people, many of whom read little if anything, that they were intent on portraying. Nevertheless, Lamming defends the novel, explaining its function thus:

> I do not know whether literary scholars make the connection, but one of the functions of the novel in the Caribbean is to serve as a

form of social history. The novelist thus becomes one of the more serious social historians by bringing to attention the interior lives of men and women who were never thought to be sufficiently important for their thoughts and feelings to be registered.[13]

It is interesting that Lamming valorises fiction as a form of social history whereas Gladwell chooses autobiography to particularise her experience.

West Indian Women and the Tradition of Autobiography

Gladwell's choice to depict her experiences in an autobiography, rather than a novel, points up a rather different sense of personal ambition to that of her male contemporaries. Aspiring West Indian writers of the period were busy producing the fiction, drama and poetry that would create a new field of West Indian literature. Gladwell's choice of genre signals the desire to expose injustices and denials in the material world, but equally important is the question of how these injustices challenge her deeply held Christian beliefs. In this respect, her autobiography connects to the spiritual journey which Saint Augustine describes in *Confessions* (c. AD 398–400). As Linda Anderson tells us, Augustine's *Confessions* 'is often thought of as the origin of modern Western autobiography, both in the sense of marking a historical beginning and of setting up a model for other, later texts'.[14] Anderson cites George Gusforf's work to describe how Augustine expresses 'the Christian imperative to the confession of sins and [...] that inward-turning gaze which is the origin and basis of autobiography'.[15] Spirituality and the 'inward-turning gaze' infuse Gladwell's autobiography, speaking to and comforting black Christians at a time when many of them were being treated as a sub-species of humanity. At this particular historical moment, Gladwell's choice to write a spiritual autobiography was a radical departure. With few female role models, in part a feature of West Indian patriarchy, women found it difficult to imagine themselves as writers or to aspire, as their male contemporaries did, to express their situation imaginatively through literature. Gladwell's book refutes the conditions of women writers' self-imposed silence.

Women writers often use the autobiographical, cast in fiction such as Merle Hodge's *Crick Crack, Monkey* (1970) and *For the Life of Laetitia* (1993), to reveal a deeply personal experience that would otherwise be absent from the historical record. Both fiction and autobiography demand a high level of commitment and literary skill. One explanation offered to me for the paucity of novels by Caribbean women was the assumption that women lacked the material means, the space, the time and/or the skill, to engage in the demands presented by such a sustained piece of writing. Women, it is often advanced, have the time to scribble a poem at the kitchen table, but their lives do not allow for writing anything of substance. An example like *Brown Face, Big Master* clearly challenges this particular explanation for Caribbean women writers' occlusion, since autobiographies demand an equally sustained commitment and involve similar creative decisions and formulations.

Novels provide the imaginative scope to play out fantasies – what Freud identified as the distinct ability of the creative writer to use writing as a form of wish-fulfilment or day-dreaming.[16] An autobiography is no less fictive in that it will entail an element of recasting and wish-fulfilment in its construction. Indeed, this literary opportunity to interrogate memory and to re-play a past, with significant others reconstructed through a later understanding, may supply the prime motivation for its production. But if autobiographies use memory creatively, then they do so under different terms. Novel writing enables the writers to place themselves behind the protective shield of 'this is fiction' and novelists may choose to put a distance between the material and their own life histories. Autobiographies must own up to the record of experience, and premise that record on a shared expectation ('a contract' between reader and writer) that it is based, however selectively, on a version of a 'truth' and is not an arbitrarily fantastic creation. Philippe Lejeune explains that 'the author of an autobiography implicitly declares that he is the person he says he is and that the author and the protagonist are the same.'[17] The way that this declaration is received is inevitably gendered; Saint Augustine established the genre of autobiography as a masculine imperative. Nevertheless, in generic terms, it is the owning and naming of the protagonist's experience that provides the critical difference between novels and autobiographies. Of course, I am simplifying a body of feminist critical thinking which has theorised, with increasing sophistication, the use of memory and narrative in women's autobiography.

As Linda Anderson writes 'memory is not static'; it may '[...] provide a space in which the subject can create herself.' She goes on to explain that memory 'contains a future we have yet to gain access to'.[18] To say that autobiographies are about the subject's future may seem contradictory, but for the young Gladwell her interrogation of the past inevitably poses the question of what the future holds for someone with knowledge of this past: put simply as 'we write towards a future which we do not know but which may eventually know us differently.'[19] As a young unknown woman, Gladwell was a long way from anticipating her autobiographical deathbed. Instead her work pre-empts a postmodernist emphasis on the future rather than the past, described by Laura Marcus as 'a mode in which the self or selfs are made ready for the future'.[20]

In order to make the self 'ready for the future', Gladwell must confront and construct her history. In *Historical Thought and Literary Representation in West Indian Literature*, Nana Wilson-Tagoe asks: 'What would history be like if it were seen through the eyes of women and ordered by values they define?'[21] Gladwell's text responds with a version of history which challenges those Caribbean literary histories, like Wilson Tagoe's, that deny her generation a dynamic literary space. Wilson-Tagoe explains away all too easily earlier Caribbean women writers' invisibility to their maintainence of the African-oral tradition which, she writes, left them '[d]isadvantaged educationally and often unable to express their experiences in the new languages and forms of representation'.[22] This familiar argument subsumes all Caribbean women writers, even those highly literate ones like Gladwell, into a semi-literate class. It is a pity that Wilson-Tagoe's important project avoids the problematic but significant tradition of the autobiography as *the* imaginative literary genre associated with many early black women writers.[23] As Laura Marcus explains:

> As a hybrid form, autobiography unsettles distinctions, including the division between self and other. In this sense, it becomes a

> destabilising form of writing and knowledge [where the] inner of
> the self is constituted as both a sacred place and a site of danger.[24]

Gladwell's autobiography is an example of a strange and powerful
hybrid with the power to transform objects of history into *the* historical subject of change. The strength of Gladwell's autobiography lies in her ability to represent a unique experience which lays
no claim to generality or historical authenticity. Yet it is paradox-
ically the revelation of a uniquely individual perspective which
may contribute to a recasting of 'official', male-centered, and
monumental versions of history. Autobiographies don't claim to
be history but are self-evidently the written testimonies of a wilful
memory, reconstructed using the conventional narrative strat-
egies of characterisation, temporality, suspense and point-
of-view. If autobiographies are to be used as historical evidence,
then selectivity and partiality must be confronted by reading the
testimonies against a range of contemporary historical sources.

The writing and publication of *Brown Face, Big Master* was an
act of bravery and self-determination. In respect of West Indian
women writers in the 1960s, this may appear in itself contradictory since many women writers suffered from determined
attempts to undermine their feelings of self-worth. Some of
Gladwell's contemporaries (for example Merle Hodge, Barbara
Ferland, Christine Craig) were affected by a lack of self-esteem,
an inability to perceive themselves as 'writers', and this must have
prevented them from advancing their career through a greater
quantity of published work. Anderson quotes Nancy Miller on
this issue:

> Because women have not had the same historical relation of iden-
> tity to origin, institution, production that men have had, they have
> not, I think, (collectively) felt burdened by too much Self, Ego,
> Cogito etc.[25]

Usually, autobiographies are the province of the famous or the
notorious, of those 'burdened' with fully inflated egos and those
deemed to have had extraordinary lives or have extraordinary talents.
But an autobiography from an unknown woman functions differently
to record the otherwise unknown material details of her everyday life.

Such an autobiography is, therefore, a supreme act of defiance (and revenge) which reclaims and remakes a damaged identity.

Gladwell's choice of form connects to one of the earliest known literary sources by a West Indian woman (*The History of Mary Prince, a West Indian Slave, Related by Herself* published in 1831). Significantly, she writes not as a victim but as a highly educated, relatively privileged, 'coloured', and middle-class, female. In terms of the Caribbean, the privilege of this position depicts an experience which may be overlooked by postcolonial literary historians intent on reclaiming a subaltern's perspective. Women writers are ever in danger of being overlooked if their voices are seen to be part of that minority perspective of colonialists or are in any way complicit, by way of their race, class or skin colour, with the power structures of a former planter society. Colonial women writers of the 1940s and 1950s sometimes fall into this category. Whereas Gladwell's African-Caribbean genealogy is not in question, an autobiography from a white planter-class woman is an unlikely subject for recuperation. The little known autobiography by Lucille Iremonger, *Yes My Darling Daughter* (1964) exemplifies Evelyn O'Callaghan's assessment:

> With neither blackness, nor money and 'Englishness' as a passport to identity, she's a lonely, withdrawn, isolated and marginal figure, subject to cruel paradoxes – such as having privileges with virtually no power, or being oppressed without the support and solidarity of fellow victims.[26]

However, as O'Callaghan reminds us, for black, white, male or female, this is the desperate situation which provides the genesis for writing in exile:

> Interestingly, alienation (produced by historical and societal factors) leading to temporary or permanent exile and thus to artistic creation for these women writers, follows the same pattern as the male West Indian writer's well documented journey in a quest of a literary identity. Thus the factors that drive characters like Stella, Natalie and Em [in Phyllis Shand Allrey's *The Orchid House*] to permanent, wandering exile and Antoinette [in Jean Rhys' *Wide Sargasso Sea*] to madness, seem to have been channelled into creative literary production by their authors.[27]

This is a literary production stimulated by what Salman Rushdie describes as the migrant writer's capacity for a 'double perspective: because they, we, are at one and the same time insiders and outsiders in this society. This stereoscopic vision is perhaps what we can offer in place of "whole sight" '.[28] Being an outsider in society is indisputably gendered in certain ways, but alienation, despair and the need to stabilise an identity in crisis, affects men and women with equal force. Julia Kristeva asserts that it is the *situation* of loss and uncertainty that provides the prerequisite to the act of creative writing:

> I would say that the creative act is released by an experience of depression without which we would not call into question the stability of meaning or the banality of expression. A writer must at one time or another have been in a situation of loss – of ties, of meaning – in order to write.
>
> There is nevertheless something paradoxical about a writer, who experiences depression in its most acute and dramatic form, but who also has the possibility of lifting her/himself out of it.[29]

We see that Gladwell, like most migrant writers, experiences this paradox in that she suffers the depression associated with severance from relatively stable social connections in Jamaica but, in England, she too acquires the 'double perspective' and the need to find a means to 'lift herself out of it'.

My work suggests that the most significant genre of writing to emerge from women in this period was not fiction, but *autobiography*, set both in the colonial West Indies and in post-war Britain. Exiled West Indian women writers, then, are creative in the post-war period but are often overlooked for complex reasons to do with genre, the publishing industry and the way that these intersect with the academy, patriarchy and liberal politics. If Gladwell needed to 'lift herself out' of her alienation and despair then she chose to do this through the creative act of life writing. She does not seem to have had any desire to write fiction. In the text, she states that her prime motivation for writing was precisely that she owned and understood that experience.

Pioneering writer and teacher Beryl Gilroy, was also compelled towards the autobiographical when she wrote her collection of Afro-

Guyanese reminiscences, *Sunlight on Sweet Water*, in the late 1960s. She was advised to fictionalise the work for publication:

> I wrote those pieces for my children. Actually, I didn't write them – I typed them up. I took the time to take them into college and type them so they could be copied. And I sent them everywhere and nobody wanted it. […] They weren't publishing pieces that didn't fictionalise people and I said I can't fictionalise all these people. So I kept it.[30]

Significantly, although the characters she writes about are as compelling as any in fiction, she refused to weld them together in the picaresque style of Selvon's *The Lonely Londoners* and the book had to wait 30 years to find a publisher. She was indignant that the original readers failed to recognise the significance of the stories. Although Gilroy's reminiscences are set in the vastly different landscape of a pre-independent British Guiana, they are in many ways like Flora Thompson's social, economic and cultural account of pre-industrial Oxfordshire, published as *Lark Rise to Candleford*. Gilroy and Thompson were both engaged in a form of literary archaeology, recording the fragments of a world that has disappeared irretrievably.[31] It is ironic that Oxford University Press wished to take *Lark Rise* as an autobiography rather than fiction, but Thompson fictionalised her world in order to protect the village inhabitants' privacy. Gilroy, on the other hand, was separated in time and space from British Guiana; she explicitly named the people of her childhood, eulogising them for her own children and for a generation of children who might never visit the Caribbean and its lost rural community. Gilroy's concern was that her own urbanite children, Paul (Gilroy) and Darla, would never know of the vivid lifestyle of their African-Caribbean ancestors except through her reminiscences. The village of her childhood was no better preserved than Thompson's 19th century Candleford Green. As Gilroy explains in her 1990 Preface:

> By no stretch of the imagination could my two children growing up in a London suburb construct images of my childhood in the then British Guiana, my grandparents or their innumerable friends and acquaintances. […] for my children Guyana was remote and strange in a way that London was not. So I have tried to recapture

times, people, and occasions in these sketches, which I am happy
to say delighted and informed my children and I hope will do the
same for my grandchildren and their friends.[32]

Diasporic female identity quests may stimulate the need to write
for children born in a different age and a different country, but,
equally, women writers problematise relationships with parents
and grandparents from the 'other world' of their own childhood.
Carolyn Steedman's *Landscape for a Good Woman* (1986),
Rachel Manley's *Drumblair* (1997) and *Slipstream* (2000), and
Lorna Sage's *Bad Blood* (2000) are critically acclaimed examples
of this type of writing. Gladwell also writes to her mother and for
her children. This point will prove to be important to the discussion of *Brown Face, Big Master* that follows.

The Spiritual Quest: *Brown Face, Big Master*

Andrew Salkey is noted for encouraging new writers, and in 1969
he reviewed *Brown Face, Big Master*, clearly expecting that it
would become a classic in the blooming West Indian corpus. He
had this to say about the paucity of women writers in this corpus
at the time:

> West Indian writing has to date only three well-known published
> women writers; Louise Bennett, Ada Quayle and Sylvia Wynter. A
> fourth is the distinguished historian Dr Elsa Goveia who has pub-
> lished books on West Indian history but has not written either
> fiction or autobiography. Special attention, then, ought to be paid
> to the publication of *Brown Face, Big Master* by Joyce Gladwell.[33]

The 'special attention' that Salkey called for was prophetic, as was his
claim that 'Joyce Gladwell is a writer of intense feeling and integrity.
Her story is engagingly written, well-paced and sincere. It should
gain her a substantial readership in Britain and the West Indies'.[34]
Salkey was an influential member of the male cohort of writers that
established the 'West Indian on the Final Passage' as a significant literary development. He recognised that Gladwell's 'Woman Version'
insight into colonial Jamaica and migration to London in the 1950s
was a rare accomplishment.[35] Salkey correctly predicted that
Gladwell's autobiography would gain 'a substantial [worldwide]

readership' but there were complex forces at work which contributed to its later suppression. Consequently, at the turn of the twenty-first century very few scholars of Caribbean literature would now be familiar with the object of Salkey's praise. In the following discussion I wish to follow the book's trajectory, tracing its popularity and censorship in the late 1960s, to its present obscurity. As an exercise in literary sociology, we might also consider it excellent material for a case study of how West Indian women's literary expression is lost. Having researched the conditions which contributed to a paucity of West Indian women's writing from 1960s, the important questions for me are: why would a young, self-effacing and completely unknown Jamaican woman write a full-length autobiography and, how did it come to be published? Why did a West Indian woman, the traditional carrier of non-literary forms of an oral tradition, choose to publish her experience in a flawless standard English prose? All this needs explaining. Fortunately, it is rare that we have the process of creation so thoroughly documented as we do in the case of *Brown Face, Big Master*.

In 1953, the author was a 22-year-old student with a place at London University to study psychology in a department whose faculty included the eminent scientist H.J. Eysenck. When she stepped off a West Indian banana boat she had no manuscript in her luggage, nor any aspirations towards becoming a full-time writer, as her contemporaries Lamming, Selvon and Naipaul had done. Few women writers, with the possible exception of Sylvia Wynter, who published *The Hills of Hebron* in 1962, were likely to arrive with manuscripts destined for publication in their luggage. In the late 1950s, even in metropolitan London, it would have been highly unusual for a woman to think in terms of a writing career. And yet Gladwell succeeded in publishing a full-length autobiography at a time when West Indian women writers (of African-, Indian- and Chinese-Caribbean origins) were largely invisible. It confronted the thorny construct of a gendered colonial identity in an act of defiance. Given the particular historical circumstances in which the book was written, seeing the manuscript through to publication required a sustained level of literary skill which would insist that aesthetic accomplishment was as important as the author's need to re-tell her experience. Gladwell was concerned that, as Salkey put it, the book be 'engagingly written'. Additionally, the act of writing required a sustained level of self-esteem which was, in respect of Gladwell, paradoxical. She writes of the lasting effects of her boarding school education '[…] my self-esteem was damaged. I suffer still. The feelings of self-condemnation to which I am subject by nature were so reinforced by the moral tyranny at St Hilary's that they prevail even in adulthood'.[36] That she found the courage to write about these feelings in the liminal and creative space of the metropolis is of course significant; the experience of being such a long way from home, and in such an unexpectedly hostile environment, provided the 'situation of loss' that Kristeva claims ignites a creative spark.

Brown Face, Big Master was published as a religious book but some of the material caused a storm on its first and only print run in 1969. Booksellers in Northern Ireland and South Africa were concerned that Gladwell's frank descriptions of sexual assault, racism and mixed-race relationships might offend some of their readers and they refused to sell it. The work then fell into obscurity, so that subsequently it has remained outside of the Caribbean literary recuperative project. When I found this book in 1995, I needed to understand its provenance, its reception, its occlusion, and it seemed impossible to answer important questions without gaining access to information which could only be supplied by the book's author. After a period of two years and much help from Bridget Jones and Gertrud Aub-Buscher, I traced the author to an address in Canada. What follows is dependent upon personal information generously supplied by Joyce Gladwell. The contextual evidence enables meaningful connections to be made between the text, the historical conditions of its production, its reception in 1969, and its present obscurity. One of the author's letters explained, not only the circumstances in which the text came to be lost, but also the circumstances of its wide distribution at the time, its reception and its eventual censorship:

> IVP [the press of the Inter-Varsity Christian Fellowship] has a wide distribution system through Christian booksellers in all parts of the world. I received responses from Australia, India, Hong

Kong, the Philippines as well as the USA, the United Kingdom and the Caribbean. The book was refused by South African book-sellers because of the presentation of a racially mixed marriage, and refused in Northern Ireland because my sexual encounter with the ship's doctor was considered pornographic.

The book was serialised in the *Daily Gleaner* in Jamaica.

I read excerpts on the BBC and was interviewed by Southern Television in England. The 21,000 copies were sold out by 1974.[37]

At the time of its publication, then, the book was held to be both aesthetically accomplished and groundbreaking, but when it sold out it was never reprinted. IVP had world-wide distribution in the 1960s and is still trading through its USA and UK companies. The website tells us that 'IVP is the publishing wing of the Universities and Colleges Christian Fellowship. Publishing began between the two world wars, born of a need for good quality Bible-based literature to resource preachers, students and thinking Christians.'[38] Having sold out of its 21,000 copies of *Brown Face, Big Master* by 1974, it seems likely that the decision not to reprint the book was a matter of its reception rather than its evident saleability.

Marcus suggests that autobiography, and particularly women's autobiography, is especially capable of destabilising racial, imperial, patriarchal authority in its 'disclosure of insider secrets'.[39] Clearly many readers validated Gladwell's 'disclosure' in their letters to the author. As part of that lost archive of colonial literature, the book may now be recovered by 'the troubled theoretical values of postcoloniality'. As Leela Gandhi writes: 'postcolonial theory inevitably commits itself to a complex project of historical and psychological "recovery" '.[40]

The first stage in this procedure is to retrieve the artefacts from a colonial past which offer up new understandings to the agents of postcolonial enquiry. On the back cover of the 1969 edition of *Brown Face, Big Master*, the book is advertised as a work that explores 'some of the major social problems of our time – race, colour, human relationships, mixed marriage, the search for God'. Its publication, by the Inter-Varsity Christian Fellowship, was timely and responded to a British media which cast migrants as the source of social 'problems'.

West Indian students who arrived with scholarships, or who were privately funded, were differently orientated to the majority of migrants who came to Britain for work; when they returned home, their British experience – of education, of racism, of resistance – was critical to the revolution which took place in Caribbean arts, politics and education. Anne Walmsley explains how students, like Gladwell, continued to be drawn to the metropolis: 'In the 1960s, the decade of independence, ties between Britain and her former colonies were still strong. The cream of graduates from the University of the West Indies still came to Britain for postgraduate study.'[41] It was this quasi-permanent West Indian student presence, with its intellectual and creative ferment, that stimulated Andrew Salkey, John La Rose and Edward Kamau Brathwaite to form The Caribbean Artists Movement (1966–1972). Gladwell was at university before the formation of The Caribbean Artists Movement and her support networks were religious rather than artistic. By the time she was writing her book, she was isolated as a housewife and mother in Southampton with no access to the male-centred networks that aided her contemporaries. For the majority of West Indians arriving in Britain, finding a means for *religious* expression was vitally important. Although Gladwell's crisis of faith provides the scaffold for the autobiography, she also breaks new ground in confronting issues of interracial marriage, racism and sexuality, exposing much that would usually remain within the protected private domain of the West Indian family.

Gladwell's autobiography results from the junction of two very vital impulses: the need to 'tell' her story and the need to affirm her faith in what was essentially a spiritual quest. The work came into being primarily to document a journey towards greater understanding of the author's struggles to comply with family expectations, and the depression and isolation that British racism brought in the early years of her mixed marriage, to a point where she can accept the 'Big Master' of Christian faith. *Brown Face, Big Master* depicts very explicitly how Gladwell faces the contradictions of a colonial childhood, the stifling atmosphere of a Jamaican boarding school, and the psychological fragmentation incurred by transfer, in 1953, from rural Jamaica to London University. The book is historically significant in that it evidences some important changes in Jamaican and Black British history which are part of a 'lost' and gendered history of Caribbean literary expression.

Joyce Nation, as she was then, was born one of twins, in 1931 in Mandeville in the parish of Manchester. Both parents were teachers who had moved away from their native parish to settle and work in St Catherine in the small farming district of Harewood. She begins her autobiography in this quiet and 'very beautiful' rural Jamaica, describing this as the 'scene of [her] happy childhood' (p.51). Writing in exile, in the comparatively drab surroundings of post-war Southampton, she revels in the colours and senses of her childhood haunts and the opening description is packed with nostalgia for a lost world that might be fixed in her imagination. She begins her second paragraph with a simple verbless sentence: 'And the quietness.' The ellipsis and the emphasis are poetic, conveying homesickness. In the early part of the autobiography, the richness of the childhood landscape contrasts with a sense of self-containment and isolation. The girls have little access to the type of temporary relief from parental 'guidance' that young children often acquire through their peers and their relationships with teachers at school. For Joyce and her sister, Faith, school was an extension of home. They were clearly marked as different from local children because both parents taught at the school and their father was the head teacher:

> If I felt my childhood was deprived it is in this sense: that we lacked gay abandon, romping childish fun and the companionship of equals. [...] At school, the other children did not treat us as equals; our father was the head teacher and we were 'teacher daughter', to be picked for the side in games because of our social position, not our prowess, to be asked favours, not to be bosom friends. (p.52)

The twins lived an ambivalent social existence, in daily contact with the local black community, but rarely mixing with children of their own age. Their knowledge of the world came in part from eavesdropping on their father's discussions with the local people who called for his help and advice. They also learned to substitute reading for the friendships that they might have developed had they not been separated from other children in the play-yard.

From the beginning of the autobiography, we understand that the girls spend their early lives protected to the extent that they become unhappy 'spectators, full of brooding thoughts, seeking satisfaction from inside ourselves and conscious of a growing dissatisfaction.' (p.53). Their lives were also affected by material shortages caused by the Second World War. Children in wartime Jamaica had 'few clothes, toys, books' and there was 'no cinema, no library, not even a radio'.[42] Young girls had to be watched and protected from engaging in one of the few playful distractions available and sex outside marriage was a constant anxiety for parents, here reflected in the words of a Jamaican folksong, current at that time:

> Gal dey a school a study fi teacher
> Boy dey a bush a study fi breed her.[43]

The song warns against the unplanned pregnancy that would destroy the possibility of educational improvement. In *Brown Face, Big Master*, it is clear that Gladwell's parents share a generation's anxieties and ambitions for their children. Joyce and Faith are raised to be religious, educated and refined; and they understand that one of their goals in life should be a Christian marriage and children. Local children tantalise with stories of sexual 'deviation' but the details are quickly withdrawn: 'How often on the brink of a juicy revelation, my informant would draw back: "But ah won' tell you, for you gwine tell you mada."' (p.59). Misdemeanours are unthinkable since: 'My mother seemed to scan my every thought; she watched us and supervised every moment of our time. And God never overlooked a sin. Neither did my mother.' (p.60). Gladwell's early life becomes troubled and obsessive in a way that that her parents did not anticipate: 'Had they known, they would have feared for our sanity.' (p.60). An omnipresent God, caring but demanding, was 'knitted into the fabric of our minds.' (p.63). Providing the central dichotomy of the text, Gladwell's obsession with the demands of the 'Big Master' of her faith causes her considerable spiritual anguish, but it is undoubtedly the strength of this belief which sustains her when she becomes separated from the comfort and guidance of her parents.

Gladwell's narration displays a rhetorical device that Roland Barthes would employ self-consciously to prove a theoretical point. In his own life-writing, Barthes demonstrated that neither the subject of the autobiography, nor the past life that this subject inhabits, is in anyway unified, monumental or able to be recovered. Linda Anderson writes that Barthes, in his autobiography *Roland Barthes by Roland Barthes* (1977), rejected the use of the first person:

> Barthes, therefore, with unmistakable ostentation, not only disperses the autobiographical subject between positions or pronouns, he also rigorously eschews narrative for the fragment, using the alphabet to ensure a random ordering of autobiographical snippets or self-reflections which deny the subject both origin and destiny.[44]

Barthes took his formal experimentation to extremes, but Gladwell also allows her pronominal usage to slip, narrating sometimes as 'we', sometimes as 'I', sometimes as 'me', sometimes as 'us'. It is unclear whether she is speaking for the young Joyce, the adult Joyce, the twins or, collectively, for her generation. Like all autobiographies, the narrative comments on, evaluates and filters the past through a later understanding. It is the act of writing the autobiography that would allow conflicting elements and tensions to emerge in the course of their re-discovery. Linda Warley describes the process thus: 'the autobiography represents a personal quest where the autobiographer traces his (sic) life by organising the narrative according to significant stages.'[45] Gladwell's 'quest' to organise the significant and shaping events of her early life illustrates the impossibility of shearing off past miseries from the present. The 'real' quest for Gladwell is the release of long-repressed doubts and anger, confronting the way the present and the future are determined by the past, and confronting the mixed emotions that surface in the retelling of her childhood. This is characterised by the two following juxtaposed statements: 'where did we learn or inherit the [religious and moral] scrupulosity, the obsessiveness? Perhaps somewhere my mother had a hand in it'(p.60); and

> Perhaps, later we fought against God because we feared that, like Mama, He would limit our freedom and possess us completely.

But in finding Him eventually, we found the One who cared infinitely, though He was the 'God of the whole earth', cared for us as if there were no one else beside us. (p.61)

In the early part of the autobiography, God and mother are fused into one all-knowing, all-seeing figure and the narrative voice expresses a resentment which is at odds with an equally strong desire to convey love and respect for the narrator's mother.

Gladwell's intelligence and creativity would find limited opportunities in pre-independent Jamaica. Her social and personal development entailed a preparation for transfer to an English society that would be made familiar to her through her colonial education. However, many Caribbean writers find their experience of a colonial education system to be a deeply ambivalent source for their creativity. Gladwell is no different in this respect and her version offers us the conditions for cultural dislocation, affected by the severance of a connection with her birthplace. A sense of belonging to Jamaica is replaced by a false consciousness, achieved through superimposing a familiarity with, and attachment to, England. She understands the importance of negative and positive spatial connections in this rubric of displacement. As Warley argues: 'Spaces "speak". They are coded, meaningful signs. Spaces are permitted or taboo.'[46] Gladwell's recounts the obsessive little-Englishness of her school (based on the boarding-school, St Hilda's):

The curriculum was imported from England; the books and subject-matter were English. Even the exercise books were sent from Foyles in London. This only continued what had begun at Harewood, for at that time, even in elementary school, we learnt to read from books prepared for English schools, illustrated with pictures of rolling English wheat-fields and well-clad English children climbing over stiles. In our more advanced readers we had met reproductions of the English painters, Turner and Constable, whose muted colours seemed incredible to our eyes which were so well used to vivid sunshine, contrast of light and shade, and brilliant colours.

Also from England were the spoken accents, the niceties of behaviour and, in spite of the difference in climate, the uniform. When my sister and I began our internment there in 1943, the serge skirts had just been replaced by blue cotton tunics, but some seniors were still wearing black stockings. (pp.77)

From the outset of their expensive and privileged education, the girls of St Hilary's are taught to project their sense of self into an imaginary space. St Hilary's results are achieved through strict discipline and a system of deprivation:

> I use 'internment' deliberately. The life of the school, especially for the boarders, was cut off from the town, and indeed from everything around it – from the social and cultural mix of Jamaican life, and from communications with the outside world. We did not read the papers unless we were in the top forms, but perhaps we lost little; the day of the transistor radio was not yet and the school radio set was rarely used. We did not speak to the maids; we did not ask the daygirls to bring or buy anything for us. We wrote letters once a week. These could be written to parents, to a brother or to female friends and relatives but to no-one else without specific permission, and the addressed envelopes were checked. (p.77–8)

Gladwell must collude with a system which disrupts her sense of belonging to Jamaica. This dramatic result is achieved through features that resemble the literal 'internment' of a prison regime: limited access to forms of communication with the immediate community resulting in an isolation from people with a different life outside that of the school; censorship of the content and quantity of letters; the loss of individuality by an inappropriate uniform; and control of the flow of possessions. Gladwell's perspective on this 'internment' is at its most unstable in this section, and moves between conflicting judgements on the gains and losses incurred by her privileged education: 'I use internment deliberately' and 'but perhaps we lost little'. The adult narrator is never quite able to convince that the child's isolation was ultimately beneficial. Significantly, she mourns the loss of a Jamaican identity associated here with the eradication of her natural voice: 'The dialect had no place here [St Hilary's]. This is what I looked forward to and what my parents wanted, but when it came I had a sense of loss.' (p.78). Before Kamau Brathwaite had claimed the Jamaican idiom as 'nation language', it was exchanged for pretensions in speech that now seem quite bizarre.[47] Gladwell writes of a form of address – they 'learnt how to say "gels" for "girls"' – that Muriel Spark had parodied in 1961 in *The Prime of Miss Jean Brodie*.[48] But typically, Gladwell reflects on the consequences of 'rules for everything', at once defending and questioning the same point:

> No wonder when I emerged from the school [...] I was like some woodland creature accustomed to living underground, unhappy and unsure in the light and freedom. Yet every one of these restrictions could be justified; I myself have, on occasion, vigorously supported them. How can many live and work together smoothly without some loss of freedom? But could it have been less severe? (p.83)

The author describes this experience as taking place in 1945, a time of growing nationalism when scholarships for girls with a 'wholly Jamaican background' were on the increase, and this engendered a growing spirit of rebellion against the Anglicised tradition of the school (p.80). However, St Hilary's was spectacularly effective in alienating the girls from Jamaican language and culture, in infusing a sense of English culture, and in feeding the imperative of transfer to an English university. This was exactly what was expected of a colonial boarding school. The stripping-away of a Jamaican voice and culture enabled Joyce to be at 'ease in social contacts' on her transfer to England (p.79). The years of conformity, however, created few opportunities for independent thought and judgement. By the time she transfers to England, the narrator professes that she has achieved a certain freedom of choice (between good and evil) and an acceptance of her ancestry, but the route to this understanding has been achieved in spite of restrictions imposed by a school which would leave her vulnerable and unprepared for a post-war metropolis.

Gladwell finds herself on a banana freighter to London with twenty other passengers including the young son of Marcus Garvey. The only woman at the Captain's table, she immediately falls prey to the dishonourable intentions of the ship's English doctor. She finds herself in his cabin alone:

> I dared not make a dash for the door or resist him for fear of arousing him further – to violence perhaps. Then I remembered a novel

I had read from the sixth-form library in which the hero, finding himself alone with his beloved, was completely put off by her coldness. 'I could not take you, Mary,' he said. I proceeded like her to play dead. Quietly but very earnestly I remonstrated. To my astonishment this had no effect. He was completely absorbed in what he was doing and quite indifferent to me.

In that moment I learnt something about the relationship between men and women that I had not allowed for before: that to make love and to love could be quite separate. I had to acknowledge even in my desperation that he was a skilful love-maker but he had not the slightest regard for me or my wishes. I have never unlearnt that lesson. If the resentment and bitterness passed in time, the sadness still remains. (p.114)

Scarcely away from the protection of her mother and young Gladwell is sexually assaulted. The passage resonates with deep symbolism: the ship's passage to England; the transportation of a defenceless 'coloured' virgin; the indifference of the English doctor and the assumption that she is an object for his pleasure. Gladwell's account of her distress, and her attempt to avoid further injury, calls up images of the rapes which took place on slave ships. St Hilary's curriculum does not include the history of such colonial encounters, nor does it include any advice on managing adult sexual transactions and the only social register on sexual matters that Gladwell has had access to, a sentimental novel, is dangerously inadequate. It is because of her unfounded assumption that no man would possibly 'take' an unwilling partner – and that she simply has to 'play dead' to discourage unwanted attention – that she allows herself to be alone in the doctor's cabin at all. The novel in St Hilary's library is, typically, bound to Victorian codes of decency that turn out to be the most unreliable of fictions. She manages to avoid pregnancy by 'the merest accident – an unsuitable time of the month'. This humiliating scuffle forces a reappraisal of the social status conferred on her by her privileged boarding school upbringing. Not only has she been pitifully unprepared for cosmopolitan life; in the light of this experience, she must confront the fact that to the doctor, a representative of the metropolis, she was simply 'an easy-going coloured girl, no more.' (p.115). It is this 'pornographic' account of her sexual assault which resulted in the book being refused distribution in Northern Ireland.

By the time the author arrives in London in 1953, she is already a different person: one who is lost in a sea of pallid faces that all looked the same under a 'grey blanket of cloud which hid the sun', where, she writes, 'being a stranger is as bewildering and crippling as sudden illness.' (p.116). The experience of migration produces a 'liminal' state, characterised by the 'loss of ties' that sparks Gladwell's imagination into creative and defensive recall. As a writer, an artist, she sees everything anew, she feels everything intensely, not least the loss of Jamaica which is recalled in sharper focus. London invokes a desire for home now perceived in relation to the strange vistas of the city:

> I longed for the mountains of my own Jamaica and the warm clear nights when the sky is brilliantly packed with stars, or when the moonlight lies a rich yellow because no artificial light rivals it. I found with cruel disappointment that the sun could shine and give no warmth. (p.116)

When she gazes on the cityscape there is always the troubling shadow of Jamaica hanging over a space she begins to feel drawn to:

> I came to love the continuous sound of life that only grew less noisy in the early morning hours and the nights that were never ominous or thick with darkness as they could be at Harewood where the owl's cry was frightening, drums beat in the distance for a pocomania meeting, and the barking of dogs and the cries of night insects dominated the world of men. (pp.116–7)

Fear associated with the dark, hot, sensual, pocomanian Jamaica is contiguous with a feeling of safety produced by the cool, bland and anonymous sounds of the city.

Once settled at London University, she relates various attempts to make friends with her fellow-students but finds that they are a 'community where God was irrelevant.' (p.142). She joins the hockey team and the country-dancing set, but finds them unwelcoming. This she attributes to her lack of enthusiasm for the activities, and, feeling isolated, she turns to her sister's contacts with the Inter-Varsity Fellowship. Within this religious group, she finds warmth, and a spiritual and intellectual outlet. She also finds physical solace in the routine of sermons and prayers at Westminster Chapel, and the social activities that mark the end of the working week. However, as a privately-funded student, she is forced to move outside of this protected sphere and she takes a Saturday job on a West Ham market-stall to bolster her allowance. The journey to and from her halls of residence involve tube travel where she learns to 'glance round fearfully for "Teddy" boys', emerging with 'relief at Russell Square.' (p.118). Whilst Teddy Boys are clearly identifiable, and to some extent avoidable, Gladwell is much more distressed by verbal attacks issued when she is least prepared for them. She finds British racial tolerance thinly veneered, even the most 'civilised' of settings reveal the extent to which class prejudice will be marshalled to justify racial discrimination. For example, at a dinner party, she is wounded by the 'lack of tact and sensitivity' of a senior civil servant who proclaims that 'Colour is class':

> I had so far evaded the school encyclopaedia's claim that my colour was linked with obsession with sex, and I thought I had disproved the verdict of arrested intelligence. But here was a new limitation, fixing me till death in my place in society. (p.134)

The civil servant is describing what Hodge's Aunt Beatrice describes as 'niggeryness'; he makes plain his view that, regardless of her obvious intellectual attributes, in England she will not escape the implications of her skin colour.[49] It is very easy to see how this situation provides the conditions for Gladwell's cultural schizophrenia. It calls into question every facet of her self-image and sense of worth, 'fixing' a class position for her which she does not recognise.

At University, Gladwell also finds the importance of her Christian beliefs under attack. In the 1950s, the discipline of psychology was undergoing methodological changes and was developing a branch of psychology called behaviourism. One of Gladwell's professors, Dr. Eysenck, was instrumental in a movement to establish psychology as a branch of pure science and to cut 'the umbilical link with philosophy'. (p.129). An emphasis on scientific explanations of human behaviour would have no interest in the metaphysics of the

Christian faith. It also turns out to be an inappropriate career option for a woman, since as a relatively new discipline, it offered few openings in Jamaica at that time. But she would have faced more than seven years training for her first choice, psychiatry, which would have been at odds with other long-held expectations: 'This was an unsuitable profession for a woman, and if I pursued it, marriage would be out of the question.' In consequence, she 'gave up the ambition to be a psychiatrist', and was left with limited career choices and the study of a discipline largely devoid of theological concerns (p.127).

If the study of psychology had limited her career choices in Jamaica, the choice to go to University in itself also severely limited her marriage options back home. As she explains:

> The irony is that, in Jamaica at that time, the more educated a woman became, the smaller her chance of finding a husband. Before 1951, the year the University College of the West Indies was founded, in Jamaica, the small proportion of women who were able to go to University, had to go abroad to the U.K. or to Canada, or The States, to obtain a degree. This excursion abroad, usually during the prime dating period of her life, would set her apart from her peers, making her less, not more attractive to potential husbands, and the chances are that there would be few males left when she returned home.[50]

Hence, a British University education reduces the odds of marriage and children to a Jamaican peer. This situation was complicated by the understanding that this 'precious and wonderful relationship' should be with a partner 'who was at least the same colouring as ourselves, if not lighter'. In accordance with 'the general trend', Gladwell learns that such a marriage will be an important means of raising the family's 'social status' (p.68). This is an aspect of the colonial psyche that Frantz Fanon interrogates in *Black Skin, White Masks*: 'However painful it is for me accept this conclusion, I am obliged to state it: For the black man there is only one destiny. And it is to be white.'[51] Something of this can be achieved in part by earning 'the admiration or love of others [that] will erect a value-making superstructure on my whole vision of the world'.[52] Gladwell's textual dilemmas illustrate many aspects of Frantz Fanon's study of psychopathology. In the description below, she explains how she learns that subtle variations in skin colour transmit social 'meaning' and desire:

> Early in our lives skin colour took on meaning for us. My father would have passed for white in England, though not in Jamaica. My mother's skin was smooth chocolate. My sister and I were between them in colour, my brother was like my mother. We had relatives of every shade from black to white. Colour and shade-consciousness was a family affliction. We learnt early on that to be white was very desirable and to be black a misfortune. (p.68)

Marriage to a paler-skinned partner was the only means of ensuring that future generations would appear 'white'. In his chapter on 'The Woman of Color and The White Man', Fanon critiques Martiniquan writer Mayotte Capécia's book, *Je Suis Martiniquaise*, which was published in Paris in 1948. Fanon complains that Capécia creates a typical Antillian heroine in that 'She asks nothing, demands nothing, except a bit of whiteness in her life'. As evidence, he quotes Capécia: 'All I know is that he had blue eyes, blond hair, and a light skin and that I loved him'.[53] Fanon's frustration with a perpetuation of the colonial mindset is clearly articulated:

> Every time I have made up my mind to analyze certain kinds of behaviour, I have been unable to avoid the consideration of certain nauseating phenomena. The number of sayings, proverbs, petty rules of conduct that govern the choice of a lover in the Antilles is astounding. It is always essential to avoid falling back into the pit of niggerhood, and every woman in the Antilles, whether in a casual flirtation or in a serious affair, is determined to select the least black of the men.[54]

It was impressed upon the twins that 'falling back into the pit of niggerhood' will not happen to them. The girls must not enter into any relationship that would result in them identifying with, or bringing more blackness into, a family who had 'progressed' socially by marrying whiter skinned partners:

> It was implicit in our upbringing that we would not identify ourselves with the majority of people round us who lived in concubinage and among whom pregnancy outside a stable relationship was common. But she [mother] often told us of the daughter of a

middle-class family who had been seduced by a yard boy. This cautionary tale impressed on us that it could happen to us, but here we felt she went too far. This was the measure of my mother's success in shaping our attitudes, that we thought it unnecessary and insulting to have this story brought to our notice. (p.70)

Seeking whiteness through marriage to a white partner brings Manichean thinking into sharp relief. Binaries that are the coloniser's legacy in the West Indies become compounded by British racism, marking out fresh humiliations for the West Indian migrant. Selvon, in *The Lonely Londoners*, illustrates the strength of racist feeling which attends mixed relationships in the 1950s. Selvon's character Bart is taken home to meet the family of his white girlfriend. When the girl's father happens upon Bart sitting in his drawing room flicking through *Life* magazine he explodes into this invective:

> 'You!' the father shouted, pointing a finger at Bart, 'You! What are you doing in my house? Get out! Get out this minute!'
>
> The old Bart start to stutter about how he is a Latin American but the girl father wouldn't give him a chance.
>
> 'Get out! Get out, I say!' The father want to throw Bart out the house, because he don't want no curly haired children in the family.[55]

Clutching at straws to defend himself against the charge of being black, Bart believes that his Latin status will somehow elevate him in the father's eyes, making him less of a Negro (black) and more of a Latin (mestizo). Selvon's description is deeply rooted in the white imagination's horror of miscegenation.

Even given the shortage of Jamaican suitors, the incident with the ship's doctor convinces Gladwell that she should not engage in relationships with white men. In spite of this, she falls in love with Graham, the English-born president of the Christian Union. It seems, after all, that she will 'raise' the colour of the family through marriage to a white English academic (p.68). However, this raising of the Jamaican family status presents itself in quite the inverse relationship for Graham Gladwell's English family, for whom a 'coloured' daughter-in-law, however refined, proves unacceptable. When she meets the prospective in-laws, she is lulled into a false sense of security and finds them a pleasing embodiment of a type of 'Englishness' made familiar by St Hilary's. At their home in Kent, they appear to be agreeably tuned to her religion, and their familial routine accords exactly with her received notions of Englishness. She is charmed by their walks in the countryside, their gardening in the summer, their teas with scones and preserves, their knitting and reading by the fireside. In the generous spirit of Christianity, they welcome their son's new 'friend' as an overseas student – that is until the prospect of an engagement is announced and fears about miscegenation surface in a ugly battle of wills. What pains the author most of all is that Graham's family's objections are couched in religious and moral terms:

> But later they firmly resisted our engagement: it would be 'wrong' for their son to have a coloured child, 'wrong' for me to have a white child. […] I knew the objections to a 'mixed' marriage on social and pseudo-scientific grounds, but a moral objection was utterly new and unexpected. (p.146)

In the book, Gladwell places these in the context of the history of slavery: where 'good' Christians justified their cruelty on the grounds that 'Negroes' were – to quote the 1911 edition of the *Encyclopaedia Britannica* – 'on a lower evolutionary plane than the white man'.[56] The tone is bitter as she explains:

> Who would not baulk at the idea of an association by marriage with a sub-human species, inferior in intellect, poor in moral discernment and spiritual capacity? And the idea of having grandchildren, marked with this taint, bearing one's name, must be intolerable indeed.
>
> This was not all. Graham's parents are deeply religious, and even the bible has been used to justify racial apartheid. Had not God 'fixed the bounds of the peoples'? (p.147)

She fears that Graham's parents may view their relationship through a racial apartheid sancified even by Old Testament verses (she quotes from Deut., xxxii, 8). If we read this in the context of Southern US anti-miscegenation statutes and South African apartheid, this text does well to remind us of how painful it was for the post-war generation to resist widespread and legislated prejudice. Malcolm Gladwell, the self-reflecting third child of this union, writes of his parents' courage in a 1998 article for the *Washington Post*: "My parents' wedding pictures are radical in a way that their marriage today is not. [...] It was hard for white to marry black in the 1950s because mixed marriages were so unmistakably political'.[57] What is interesting, by way of comparison, is the way that Gladwell describes this 'radical' wedding in *Brown Face, Big Master*. Her wedding description is coded with signals of sacrifice rather than the joy; she remembers that the spring day was, even for London, unusually chill, and that the ceremony was 'teetotal'. More importantly, she chooses not to explain why the bride's family is absent, writing simply that 'none of my relatives could be with me on that day'. It seems clear that, from now on, she will be expected to depend upon 'another family and they were there with me – a spiritual family that cut across every division of race, class, colour and ability.' (p.151). Thus begins her isolation and loneliness in marriage and her continued battle to retain a spiritual guide. Nevertheless, Malcolm Gladwell is quite right to describe mixed marriage as a revolutionary act at a time when such a marriage was a life-threatening practice in South Africa. A black woman's auto-biography, which finessed anger with reasoned argument and erudi-tion, was seen as having the potential to destabilise a regime and consequently the book was also refused distribution in South Africa.

So London University had inadvertently delivered the goal of a 'good' marriage but a series of privileged educational institutions had hardly prepared a young wife for the manual drudgery of 'keeping house' or for a life where she would be perceived as an impoverished 'coloured' immigrant in the metropolis. The fact that the two roles were often symbiotic for many migrants is not lost on the author as she confronts another new self-image with historical awareness and trepidation:

> I had more practice at Latin unseens than at cooking and I was better at doing them. I found myself on my knees washing the front steps. It was not a picture of myself I liked at all. At home the maids always did this sort of job. I was ashamed to find how much it mattered to me to do these menial tasks myself. (p.152)

The 'picture' that the narrator objects to, is characteristic of the class-shift that many migrants experience on transfer to the metropolis. West Indians who ran households with servants at home were shocked to find a white British working class that they had little idea existed. And Gladwell feels herself enslaved by the upkeep of a series of damp London flats. Depression ensues and she experiences a type of spirit thievery where she feels herself to be 'part dead in a world of walking dead' (p.153). She is soon to be cast again, this time as a pregnant mulatto, and the object of a style of medical scrutiny which owes much to a racialised nineteenth century 'scientific' discourse: 'I was the subject of a seminar held within my hearing, in which my trouble was referred to as the logical outcome of malnutrition to be expected in someone from an underdeveloped country!' (p.155).

The autobiography may help to heal the fragmented psyche of a self-image at odds with an alter ego constructed out of a racist discourse. These racist encounters, often nuanced as they are, are a source of enormous pain at a time when the author is cut off from a world which validated her self-worth and which would shore up the healthy image. As the text comes to a close the narrator reflects on the train of events which have brought her to the brink of a complete breakdown. She revisits her despair, as she writes 'What had become of the person I thought I was – confident and independent? I had become a child again, dependent, tearful, anxious, needing support and help. I needed my mother as I had not needed her during my years away from her as a student.' (p.156). Like many West Indians in the diasporas of 1950s, she is a child thousands of miles from a mother for whom, ironically, she had fulfilled every ambition.

Gladwell's autobiography was written between 1963 and 1967 when she was living with her young family on a housing estate in Southampton. She describes an incident which may have provided the catalyst for her writing. The act of having to wave off her husband and young children to the taunt of 'Nigger!' renews the terror of non-acceptance from which she cannot escape in 1960s Britain. It is, once again, the charge of 'niggeriness' that is so humiliating:

> Three months later [after the birth of her third child Malcolm] on a
> Sunday afternoon I stood at my front door waving to Graham and the
> older children as they set off for a walk. … At that moment a boy went
> by on a bicycle and shouted at me 'Nigger!' Quickly I glanced at
> Graham and the children, hoping they had not heard him, and then
> I turned indoors, my heart and mind in turmoil. A poisoned arrow
> had found its mark, a ghost from the past had visited me, and I was
> unprepared and vulnerable. The picture I had built up of an accept-
> ing community vanished. […] I was hurt and I was angry and I had to
> find expression for my raging feelings. (p.178–9)

She must have brooded on her resources and concluded that she
simply had no other means of correcting that false self-image, and
the fear she confronted on a daily basis, than to 'write back' to the
people around her, specifically her neighbours and in-laws, in
order that they 'would know who I was'.[58] And it is clear from
Malcolm Gladwell's article, aptly entitled 'Lost in the Middle',
that the autobiography is a palliative for his memory; he was that
baby in the incident of racial abuse which is narrated above. His
mother's autobiography is an emotional and psychological resource for his own understanding. In his review of the book,
Andrew Salkey writes of Gladwell's 'sharp intuition', 'psychological perception' and 'her restless humour which she applies
therapeutically', not least for her own transnational children.[59]

It is time to return to the question posed earlier. How is it that
Joyce Gladwell, a young and completely unknown West Indian
woman, came to publish a full-length autobiography in the late
1960s? As a reader for the American publishers, Dell, wrote in
1996: 'considering who she is and when it was written', it is an
extraordinary accomplishment.[60] There are several factors
which contributed to its publication:

Gladwell continuously sought comfort through some form of
writing. Years away from home had honed her letter-writing skills,
and the pleasure she received from this motivated her to write for
publication. Nevertheless, I asked her what inspired her to write
an autobiography:

> I was driven to it by circumstance. I felt isolated in England as a
> housewife and mother. For the first 5 years of my marriage I had a

writing focus as I rewrote [a Korean author's book for the English market] 'The Seed Must Die'. When I finished it in 1963 I needed something to take its place. I also felt the need to be heard and understood by people around me, so I determined to write about myself so that my neighbours and in-laws would know who I was.[61]

Narrating her life enabled her to order and account for a period fraught with intense personal conflicts of a cultural, spiritual and material kind. It also enabled her to confront the imperial stereotype with a counter-representation: Gladwell's text provides a reverse discourse on twentieth-century Britain, which becomes the barbarian 'other' of the nineteenth-century anthropologist's record. *Brown Face, Big Master* is written by the outsider who has been denied a voice, but who has in the process acquired acute observational skills and an understanding of the processes of alienation.

At some point in this process, Gladwell faced the empty page and found the courage to write her life in order to inform, to avenge, to understand. Fanon's opening remarks in *Black Skin, White Masks* come to mind:

I do not come with timeless truths.
My consciousness is not illuminated with ultimate radiances.
Nevertheless, in complete composure, I think it would be good if certain things were said.
These things I am going to say, not shout. For it is a long time since shouting has gone out of my life.
So very long …
Why write this book? No one has asked me for it.
Especially those to whom it is directed.
Well? I reply quite calmly that there are too many idiots in the world. And having said it, I have the burden of proving it.[62]

Gladwell recognised the importance of finding a role-model when she confronted the considerable challenge of lifting herself out of a cycle of destruction and denial:

We have, until recently, been fragmented in our psyche. Writing comes out of a process of self-recognition and a search for identity and integration. This process began for me when I read Vera Bell's poem 'Ancestor on the Auction Block'. This poem forced me to confront myself. It was a profoundly formative experience in my life and writing. When a few people break ground for others as Vera Bell did for me then writing can begin to flow.[63]

Bell's poem speaks to Gladwell's despair with the variety of resilience that would enable her to proceed:

> Humiliated
> I cry to the eternal abysss
> For understanding
> Ancestor on the auction block
> Across the years your eyes meet mine
> Electric
> I am transformed
> My freedom is within myself.[64]

Inspired, she also had the educational platform, ability and tenacity to see the project through. Her literary precision can be traced to a 'love of using language'; fuelled by the encouragement she received from her father, and to the 'writing skills [...] sharpened by teachers who had high standards in the British educational tradition.'[65] Caribbean writers sometimes acknowledge that their invisibility and their lack of literary role-models are bound up in a paradox: their experience of European 'classic' literature, delivered through a colonial system of education, is a mixed blessing. As Jamaica Kincaid insists: 'Included in the bad things, you get some good things too.'[66] On this point, she uses a famous Walcott poem to illustrate the language dichotomy: it flourishes the poet's own literary skills in a way that simultaneously allows him to remonstrate against the double bind of his colonial literary legacy:

> I who am poisoned with the blood of both
> where shall I turn, divided to the vein
> I who have cursed
> The drunken officer of British rule, how choose
> Between this Africa and the English tongue I love?[67]

Fanon's insight is very helpful here: 'A man who has a language consequently possesses the world expressed and implied by that

language. […] Mastery of language affords remarkable power.'[68]
For Gladwell, it was extremely important that she flourish her
skill and her power over the coloniser's language; it was part of let-
ting them know who exactly it was that they were demeaning.

Not surprisingly, then, *Brown Face, Big Master* is a very finely
written text indeed and it warrants fresh critical and historical attention. But it also contains the usual contradictions that colonial literature offers a secular postcolonial reading. The making of a colonial
female subject entails a rigorous system of cultural imperialism. St
Hilary's, the author's parents with their ambitions, and the author
herself, collude with a hegemonic system of denial determined by
the metropolis. At the same time, it is an inescapable fact that her
rigid education nurtured a rebellious spirit, a high intellect and the
talent to write a way out of the history into a different future. It is
highly unlikely that Gladwell, as a colonial subject visiting the moth-
erland, would have felt the need to write her autobiography without
the experience of an unexpectedly alien metropolis. A generation
later Anglo-Indian writer Hanif Kureishi would write a film about
life in the drug-infested world of the metropolis and give it the wonderful title of *London Kills Me*.[69] But for Gladwell in the 1950s and
Kureishi in the 1990s the metropolis remains an equally ambivalent
space. One in which it is possible to feel violently alienated and part
of a culture of alienation at the same time. In Naipaul's *A Bend in the
River*, Salim understands how Nazruddin also comes to love the city:
'The population of Gloucester Road was cosmopolitan, always shifting, with people of all ages. […] He said it was the best street in the
world.'[70] This is a space where a city's shifting multi-ethnic population ensures that liminality is the norm. Selvon ends *The Lonely
Londoners* with a description brimming over with the romance of
metropolis: 'It was a summer night: laughter fell softly: it was the sort
of night that if you wasn't making love to a woman you feel you was
the only person in the world like that.'[71] The point here is that Selvon
has Old Moses gazing on the Thames and musing on the city as a
place of possibilities, a place where writers could exploit their double consciousness through the backward glance home and the desir-
ing gaze toward the metropolis. As Gandhi points up, 'The desire of
the coloniser for the colony is transparent enough, but how much

more difficult it is to account for the inverse longing of the colonised'.[72]

The story of the suppression of *Brown Face, Big Master* does not end with its going out of print in 1974. There have been other more recent attempts at a reissue. In 1996, a reader for the New York company, Dell, praised the book as 'by far the most brilliantly honest memoir I've read in a very long time' but went on to explain that it will 'seem dated and incomplete for today's readers'.[73] Other publishers also acknowledged the extraordinary quality and importance of the work, but predicted that there would be no readership, burying the book in a history which is monumental, completed in another time and space and unable to revise our understanding. These are market-place judgements which ignore the history of migration and the way in which such patterns have changed and formed the modern world. Fortunately, Macmillan's reprint makes this text available for re-reading in the light of feminist and postcolonial enquiry or, as Salkey did, as an important existential tract which explores notions of authenticity, agency and resistance to dogma in a way that is simply not available to us elsewhere.

Acknowledgements

I wish to acknowledge Joyce Gladwell's patient correspondence which facilitated the writing of this introduction. I also thank Professor Harry Goulbourne for lending me a copy of the book in 1995 and the late Bridget Jones and Gertrud Aub-Buscher for using their extensive network to help trace Joyce Gladwell. I am grateful to the Press of the UK Inter-Varsity Christian Fellowship for searching their archives to provide me with a copy of *Brown Face, Big Master*. I am indebted to Susan Brook and Stuart Courtman for commenting on the draft. I thank *Wasafiri* for permission to reprint some of the material in my article 'Portrait of a West Indian as a Young Writer in England', 33, (2001), 9–14.

Sandra Courtman
School of Humanities and Social Sciences
Staffordshire University

NOTES TO INTRODUCTION

1   Lorna Sage cites her grandfather's sermon notes in *Bad Blood* (London: Fourth Estate, 2000), p.83.

2   M. Keith Brooker and Dubravka Juraga, *The Caribbean Novel in English* (Jamaica: Ian Randle, Oxford: James Currey, Portsmouth: Heineman, 2001), p.60.

3   The difficulty with 'West Indian' as a form of nomenclature is explained by Evelyn O'Callaghan in her book, *Woman Version*: 'the term "West Indian" is somewhat problematic, given that it is a misnomer and inscribes the region within Columbus's ignorance.' Nevertheless, it ascribes linguistic/historical/geographical specificity to people who often choose to refer to themselves as 'West Indians'. In practice, both terms are slippery and, like Alistair Hennessy, the editor for the Warwick University Caribbean Studies series, I 'use one or the other wherever textually (and stylistically) appropriate'.

4   Marjorie Thorpe, 'Feminism and the Female Authored West Indian Novel: Paule Marshall's *Brown Girl, Brown Stones*', in *Gender in Caribbean Development*, ed. by Patricia Mohammed and Catherine Shepherd, reprint (Mona: The University of West Indies Women and Development Studies Project, 1988), p.322.

5   Carole Angier, *Jean Rhys*, rev. edn (London: Penguin, 1992; first published Deutsch, 1990), p.476.

6   'But what is indisputably true is this: that in 1945 she had a novel "half-finished", and that this was *Le Revenant*, which was the first version of *Wide Sargasso Sea*.' Angier, p.371.

7   See for example the comprehensive *Bibliography of Women Writers From the Caribbean (1831–1986)*, by Brenda F. Berrian and Aart Broek (Washington: Three Continents Press, 1989), as a source for Caribbean women's writing in a variety of published forms throughout the regions of the Caribbean.

8   Joan Anim-Addo, 'Anguish and the Absurd: Key Moments and the Emergence of New Figures of Black Womanhood', unpublished paper given to the 1996 International Conference of Caribbean Women Writers and Scholars, 26 April 1996, Florida International University, Miami.

9   Kenneth Ramchand's appendix to his second edition of *The West Indian Novel and its Background*, published in 1985, cites 27 novels by West Indian women. This figure reflects the recovery of women's novels since his first edition, including Rhys's novels of the 1920s and 1930s, and women's presence as novelists was also aided by Ramchand's extension of the period from 1967 to 1982.

10 Maya Jaggi, 'Two hundred years of black bestsellers' and 'The New Brits on the Block', *Guardian*, 13 July 1996, p.31.

11 See also Joan Anim-Addo, ed., *Framing the Word: Gender and Genre in Caribbean Women's Writing* (London: Whiting and Birch, 1996), and *The Routledge Reader in Caribbean Literature*, ed. by Alison Donnell and Sarah Lawson Welsh, (London: Routledge, 1996).

12 Daryl Cumber Dance, *New World Adams: Conversations with Contemporary West Indian Writers* (Leeds: Peepal Tree, 1984), p.118.

13 George Lamming, 'Concepts of the Caribbean' in *Frontiers of Caribbean Literature in English*, ed. Frank Birbalsingh, (London: Macmillan Caribbean, 1996), p.5.

14 Linda Anderson, *Autobiography* (London: Routledge, 2001) p.18

15 Anderson, *Autobiography*, p.19.

16 See *On Freud's 'Creative writers and day-dreaming'*, ed. by Ethel Spector Person, Peter Fonagy, Servulo Augusto Figueira (New Haven: Yale University Press, 1995).

17 Cited in Anderson, *Autobiography*, p.3.

18 Linda Anderson, *Women and Autobiography in the Twentieth Century: Remembered Futures* (London: Prentice Hall, 1997), p.12.

19 Anderson, *Women and Autobiography in the Twentieth Century: Remembered Futures*, p.14.

20 Laura Marcus, *Auto/biographical Discourses: Theory, Criticism, Practice* (Manchester: Manchester University Press, 1994), p.293.

21 Nana Wilson-Tagoe, *Historical Thought and Literary Representation in West Indian Literature* (Oxford: James Currey, 1998), p.234.

22 Nana Wilson-Tagoe, p.12.

23 See *Daughters of Africa* ed. by Margaret Busby, 2nd edn. (London: Vintage, 1993)

24 Marcus, p.15.

25 Anderson, *Women and Autobiography in the Twentieth Century: Remembered Futures*, p.3.

26 Evelyn O'Callaghan, 'The Outsider's Voice: White Creole Women Novelists in the Caribbean Literary Tradition', in *The Routledge*

Reader in Caribbean Literature, ed. by Alison Donnell and Sarah Lawson Welsh (London: Routledge, 1996), p.281.

27 Donnell and Lawson Welsh, p.281.

28 Salman Rushdie, *Imaginary Homelands* (London: Penguin, 1991), p.19.

29 Julia Kristeva, 'A Question of Subjectivity – an Interview', in *Modern Literary Theory: A Reader*, ed. by Philip Rice and Patricia Waugh, (London: Routledge, 1989), p.133.

30 Beryl Gilroy, telephone interview, 12 June 1995.

31 I noted a similarity between some of the practices described in *Lark Rise to Candleford* with those depicted by Beryl Gilroy's in her Guyanese reminiscences, *Sunlight on Sweet Water* (Leeds: Peepal Tree, 1994). We discussed the fact that her own Afro-Guyanese village maintained similar rituals to those depicted by Thompson, for example, the circulation of the 'baby-box', containing clothes and other items, which was passed on to the next woman in the village who was about to give birth. See Flora Thompson, *Lark Rise to Candleford*, rev. edn (London: Penguin, 1995).

32 Beryl Gilroy, Preface, *Sunlight on Sweet Water* (Leeds: Peepal Tree, 1994)

33 Andrew Salkey, '*Brown Face, Big Master*', review of *Brown Face, Big Master* by Joyce Gladwell, *Caribbean Magazine*, 21 (1969), [n.p].

34 Salkey, *Caribbean Magazine*, [n.p].

35 Evelyn O'Callaghan (and others) have written on the invisibility of West Indian women writers in the 1970s: 'I was under the impression that there were no women writers from the region apart from Jean Rhys, *and* there was some reservation about her'. Evelyn O'Callaghan, *Woman Version: Theoretical Approaches to West Indian Fiction by Women* (London: Macmillan, 1993), p.1.

36 Joyce Gladwell, *Brown Face, Big Master* (London: Inter-Varsity Press, 1969), p. 39 (this edition, p. 84). All further references are to the Macmillan Caribbean Classics edition and appear as page numbers in the text.

37 Joyce Gladwell, letter to the author, 7 November 1996.

38 IVP online, http://www.ivpbooks.com/html, internet. 8 December, 2001.

39 Marcus, p.13.

40 Leela Gandhi, *Postcolonial Theory: A Critical Introduction* (Edinburgh: Edinburgh University Press, 1998), p.8.

41 Anne Walmsley, *The Caribbean Artists Movement, 1966–1972* (London: New Beacon Books, 1992), p.xvii.

42 Joyce Gladwell, email to the author, 14 October 2001.

43 Joyce Gladwell, email to the author, 14 October 2001.

44 Linda Anderson, *Autobiography* (London: Routledge, 2001), pp.70–71.

45 Linda Warley, 'Locating the Subject of Post-Colonial Autobiography,' *Kunapipi*, 15.1 (1993), 23–31 (p.24).

46 Warley, p.25.

47 J. Michael Dash, 'Edward Kamau Brathwaite', in *West Indian Literature*, ed. by Bruce King, 2nd edn. (London: Macmillan, 1995), p.208.

48 In *The Prime of Miss Jean Brodie* (London: Macmillan, 1961), Muriel Spark satirises a Scottish private girls' school where the protagonist, teacher Miss Brodie, speaks to her 'gels'.

49 Merle Hodge, *Crick Crack, Monkey* (London: Heinemann, 1981), p.95

50 Joyce Gladwell, email to the author, 14 October 2001.

51 Frantz Fanon, *Black Skin, White Masks*, (London: Pluto Press, 1986; first published 1952), p.12.

52 Fanon, p.41.

53 Fanon, p.42.

54 Fanon, p.47.

55 Sam Selvon, *The Lonely Londoners* (Harlow: Longman, 1985), p.65.

56 This quotation is taken from the entry under the headword 'Negro' in *The Encyclopaedia Britannica: A Dictionary of Arts, Sciences, Literature and General Information*, Eleventh Edn., Vol. XIX, (Cambridge: Cambridge University Press, 1911), pp.344–346.

57 Malcolm Gladwell, 'Lost in the Middle', *Washington Post*, 17 May 1998, online http:www.washingtonpost.com/wp-srv/national/longterm/middleground/gladwell.htm, 15.09.99. Malcolm Gladwell, also dedicates his book, *The Tipping Point* (New York: Little Brown, 2000) to his parents and writes that 'I owe special thanks to […] my mother, Joyce Gladwell, who is and always will be my favourite writer'.

58 Joyce Gladwell, letter to the author, 22 November 1996.

59 Andrew Salkey, *Caribbean Magazine*, [n.p].

60 Cherise Davis Grant of Dell Publishers, letter to Tina Bennett of Janklow & Nesbit Associates New York, 22 July 1996.

61 Joyce Gladwell, letter to the author, 22 November 1996.

62 Fanon, p.9.

63 Joyce Gladwell, letter to the author, 22 November 1996.

64 Vera Bell, 'Ancestor on the Auction Block' in *West Indian Poetry: An Anthology for Schools*, ed. by Kenneth Ramchand and Cecil Gray, (London: Longman Caribbean, 1971), pp.106–107.

65 Joyce Gladwell, letter to the author, 22 November 1996.

66 Jamaica Kincaid said 'My writing is about the relationship between the island [Antigua] and the Mother Country [...] It was better for me to have read Charlotte Brontë than Maya Angelou because Charlotte Brontë is a better writer'. Kincaid, Jamaica, public interview with Daryl Pinckney, Cheltenham Literary Festival, 15 October 1996.

67 Kincaid makes this point about Walcott's 'A Far Cry from Africa', in *Frontiers of Caribbean Literature in English*, ed. by Frank Birbalsingh (London: Macmillan, 1996), p.148.

68 Fanon, p.18.

69 Hanif Kureishi, *London Kills Me* (London: Faber, 1991).

70 V.S. Naipaul, *A Bend in the River* (London: Penguin, 1980), p.248.

71 Selvon, p.142.

72 Gandhi, p.11.

73 Cherise Davis Grant of Dell Publishers, letter to Tina Bennett of Janklow & Nesbit Associates New York, 22 July 1996.

SELECT BIBLIOGRAPHY

Anderson, Linda, *Autobiography* (London: Routledge, 2001)

——*Women and Autobiography in the Twentieth Century: Remembered Futures* (Prentice Hall, 1997)

Angier, Carole, *Jean Rhys*, rev. edn (London: Penguin, 1992; first published Deutsch, 1990)

Anim-Addo, Joan, ed., *Framing the Word: Gender and Genre in Caribbean Women's Writing* (London: Whiting and Birch, 1996)

Benstock, Shari, ed., *Theory and Practice of Women's Autobiographical Writings* (Chapel Hill, University of North Carolina Press, 1988)

Berrian, Brenda F. and Broek; Aart, *Bibliography of Women Writers From the Caribbean (1831–1986)*, (Washington: Three Continents Press, 1989

Birbalsingh, Frank, ed. *Frontiers of Caribbean Literature in English*, (Oxford: Macmillan Caribbean, 1996)

Boyce Davies, Carole and Savory, Elaine Fido, *Out of the KUMBLA* (Trenton: Africa World Press, 1990)

Brooker, M. Keith, and Juraga, Dubravka, *The Caribbean Novel in English* (Jamaica: Ian Randle, Oxford: James Currey, Portsmorth: Heineman, 2001)

Busby, Margaret, ed. *Daughters of Africa*, 2nd edn. (London: Vintage, 1993)

Capécia, Mayotte, *Je Suis Martiniquaise* (Paris: Corréa, 1948)

Conde, Mary and Lonsdale, Thorunn, eds. *Caribbean Women Writers: Fiction in English* (London: Macmillan, 1999)

Cudjoe, Selwyn R., ed. *Caribbean Women Writers: Essays from the First Conference* (Wellesley: Calaloux, 1990)

Dance, Daryl Cumber, *New World Adams: Conversations with Contemporary West Indian Writers* (Leeds: Peepal Tree, 1984)

Donnell, Alison and Lawson Welsh, Sarah, eds. *The Routledge Reader in Caribbean Literature* (London: Routledge, 1996)

Fanon, Frantz, *Black Skin, White Masks*, (London: Pluto Press, 1986)

Gandhi, Leela, *Postcolonial Theory: A Critical Introduction* (Edinburgh: Edinburgh University Press, 1998)

Gilroy, Beryl, *Sunlight on Sweet Water* (Leeds: Peepal Tree, 1994)

Gladwell, Malcolm, *The Tipping Point* (New York: Little Brown, 2000)

Hodge, Merle, *Crick Crack, Monkey* (London: Heinemann, 1981)

——, *For the Life of Laetitia* (New York: Farrar Straus Giroux, 1993)

James, C.L.R., *Minty Alley* (London: Secker and Warburg, 1936)

Joyce, James, *Portrait of an Artist as a Young Man* (New York: Viking, 1968)

King, Bruce, ed. *West Indian Literature*, rev. edn (London: Macmillan, 1995)

Kureishi, Hanif, *London Kills Me* (London: Faber, 1991)

Marcus, Laura, *Auto/biographical Discourses: Theory, Criticism, Practice* (Manchester: Manchester University Press, 1994)

Manley, Rachel, *Drumblair* (Jamaica: Ian Randle, 1996)

——, *Slipstream, A Daughter Remembers* (Jamaica, Ian Randle, 2000)

Mohammed, Patricia and Shepherd, Catherine, eds. *Gender in Caribbean Development* (Mona: The University of West Indies Women and Development Studies Project, 1988)

Naipaul, V.S., *A Bend in the River* (London: Penguin, 1980) p.248

O'Callaghan, Evelyn, *Woman Version: Theoretical Approaches to West Indian Fiction by Women* (London: Macmillan, 1993)

Olsen, Tillie, *Silences* (London: Virago Press, 1980)

Person, Ethel Spector, Fonagy, Peter, Servulo, Augusto Figueira, eds. *On Freud's 'Creative writers and day-dreaming'*, (New Haven: Yale University Press, 1995

Ramchand, Kenneth, *The West Indian Novel and its Background* (London: Faber and Faber, 1970)

—— *The West Indian Novel and its Background*, rev. edn. (London: Faber and Faber, 1985)

—— and Gray, Cecil, eds. *West Indian Poetry: An Anthology for Schools* (London: Longman Caribbean, 1971)

Rhys, Jean, *Wide Sargasso Sea* (London: André Deutsch, 1966)

Rice, Philip and Waugh, Patricia, *Modern Literary Theory: A Reader* (London: Routledge, 1989)

Rushdie, Salman, *Imaginary Homelands* (London: Penguin, 1991)

Sage, Lorna, *Bad Blood* (London: Fourth Estate, 2000)

Selvon, Sam, *The Lonely Londoners* (Harlow: Longman, 1985, first published Allen Wingate, 1956)

Spark, Muriel, *The Prime of Miss Jean Brodie* (London: Macmillan, 1961)

Stanley, Liz, *The Auto/biographical 1* (Manchester: Manchester University Press, 1992)

Steedman, Carolyn, *Past Tenses: Essays on Writing, Autobiography and History* (London: Rivers Oram Press, 1992)

——, *Landscape for a Good Woman* (London: Virago, 1986)

Swindells, Julia, *The Uses of Autobiography* (London: Taylor and Francis, 1995)

Thompson, Flora, *Lark Rise to Candleford*, rev. edn (London: Penguin, 1995)

Walmsley, Anne, *The Caribbean Artists Movement, 1966–1972* (London: New Beacon Books, 1992)

Wilson-Tagoe, Nana, *Historical Thought and Literary Representation in West Indian Literature* (Oxford: James Currey, 1998)

Wynter, Sylvia, *The Hills of Hebron* (Harlow: Longman, 1984; first published Jonathon Cape, 1962)

BROWN FACE, BIG MASTER

BY

JOYCE GLADWELL

ACKNOWLEDGEMENTS

Many friends have read the early manuscript of this book and helped by their comments and suggestions. Special acknowledgements are due to Mrs Betty Hammond who worked closely with me on the final draft, and to my husband for his indispensable support and encouragement.

Joyce Gladwell

THE church bell tolls
for the third time in a month.
A woman is sitting alone
on the stone steps of the Rectory
as the sound breaks the quietness of the countryside.
She is a servant.
Sad thoughts force themselves on her
and she speaks to herself aloud:
'So much people a dead sudden.
Suppose me go dead sudden too!
An' me a live in sin,
an' sin so sweet!'
I hear her speak
and although I am a child
I understand her problem.
She is living with a man to whom she is not married.
Down in the valley where she lives it is all right.
The people round her do the same.
Here at the Rectory it is a sin.
The church bell tolling says:
'One day you will be dead.
Perhaps it will be soon',
And then perhaps the parson will be right:
It will be hell for her if she should die in sin.

So she was caught,
like a fowl in a coop,
like a bird in a room,
like a cat in a moving car,
and for the moment she was frantic to escape.

I saw that I was like that woman
although not like her,
for I was a child
and I did not share her circumstances.
Nor would I.
At least I need never know her problem of concubinage.
But to know that what I did was counted wrong
and yet desire led me to it and held me there—
THIS. I already knew
and I would know again, again, again.
And with the knowledge I began to feel
the sense of wretchedness and helplessness
that comes with thoughts
of sin
and hell
and death.

CHAPTER I

My twin sister, my brother and I grew up in Jamaica, in a small farming district in the hills of St Catherine, named Harewood after an Earl of Harewood who owned a sugar estate there in the days of slavery. The district is very beautiful: full of colour, varied in scenery and profuse in vegetation. Day after day in our childhood we feasted our eyes on the spectacle around us with gentle pleasure. We do so still, whenever we return to Harewood, at whatever stage in our lives, however splendid the scenes from which we return. Perhaps it is the charm that attaches to any scene of happy childhood; we knew every stone and every blade of grass and we were part of them.

Certain landmarks bring their own sweet sensation – the old mango tree on the high bank, almost hidden by its broad-leaved parasite, its gnarled roots showing hideous shapes where the earth is crumbling away; the cool, sand-paved culvert, shaded by the elegant bamboo, incongruously creaking in the gentlest wind; the smell of June roses and the sight of the fragile dancing petals of lavender and white; the russet and green leaves of the star-apple tree falling to the ground where the sunshine falls in patterns through the wide leafy branches; the narrow roadway like a striped ribbon in pale yellow and green, lying at the foot of the dark blue-green mountain rising up straight beside it.

And the quietness. A great prevailing quiet broken by distant, unstartling noises – a woman singing at her washing, the 'old-man bird' crying 'Mi hoe' at intervals, a boy's shout echoing against the hills, the breeze in the coconut leaves. The steam train invaded that quiet at well-spaced intervals; occasionally, a car went by or a plane flew overhead. But these were welcome, giving excitement.

However, there were other days. From time to time the sudden drama of flood or earthquake or hurricane would shatter our security. The forked lightning and crashing thunder would draw nearer and nearer, the clear stream became a river, roaring and tumbling, murky with mud, or we would hear the ominous rumbling of an earthquake and feel sick with fear because the ground shook and there was no escape. The world of nature brought us our first disappointment: we could not take rest in her and find continued pleasure and soothing, for at any time, without warning, she might turn violent and frighten us.

My mother took great pains in bringing us up. She used to tell how carefully she ordered her life before we were born, believing that by what she did and by the books she read she would influence the babies she was carrying. While we were growing up she supplied my sister and myself with current picture-books of the English princesses; she intended us to regard the royal children and no less as our pattern.

We lived a protected, unadventurous life. Out of school we went for walks and climbed guava trees; the high spot of adventure was to climb out on a supple, bending guava limb and swing lightly to the ground. There was a stream near our home but we were not allowed to splash in it. My brother caught crayfish and 'ticki-ticki' and plunged naked in the deeper water with his friends – but not his sheltered sisters. If I felt that my childhood was deprived it is in this sense: that we lacked gay abandon, romping childish fun and the companionship of equals. A standing head of grass would invite me to throw myself into its yielding recess but I declined: 'I might get scratched or (worse) sit on a frog!' Even now I long, but would not dare, to find a private grassy slope and roll down it over and over in self-forgetfulness.

At school, the other children did not treat us as equals; our father was the head teacher and we were 'teacher daughter', to be picked for the side in games because of our social place, not our prowess; to be asked favours, not to be bosom friends. Every afternoon, after school, we looked longingly after the crowd of shouting, happy children going home together and we wished we were among them.

We lived next door to the school. Our nearest neighbours were the parson's family. He had five sons and no daughters, and so contact with them was restrained and spasmodic. When we did find one girl of our own age, attractively unlike ourselves, gay, full of schemes and active play, our friendship was discouraged. She was too forward and she had a store of doubtful stories.

We read a great deal. My father was a voracious reader. On his bookshelves we found Dickens and de Maupassant, detective tales, West Indian poetry, books on theology and philosophy. We rarely, if ever, saw the more light-hearted and colourful books designed for children. We were given a set of encyclopaedia; these we leafed through over and over again. They introduced us to a wider world of people and activities and made up for our limited experience. Our parents approved of our reading. At least they knew where we were and what we were doing and it strengthened their ambition that we would do well at school and make good as adults. But we read too much; it was a kind of drug, a substitute for a more active, involved and varied life than our parents allowed or our circumstances provided.

We varied reading with drawing and painting, sewing dolls' clothes and playing the piano. We watched my mother bake, and at intervals we cleared cupboards and helped polish furniture. But though we were always occupied, these never taxed us to the limit.

We were hardly ever involved completely with others at our own level; nothing drew us out of ourselves except the spectacle of other people's lives. We were spectators, full of brooding thoughts, seeking satisfaction from inside ourselves and conscious of a growing dissatisfaction.

World War II began when we were seven and few things could come from abroad, and so toys were scarce. I remember walking among the trees – the pear, the breadfruit, the banana tree – and breaking off small twigs with head and legs and dressing them with leaves. Not good enough. All around me were materials, dried leaves, strong strips of bark. There must be something I could do with these, something I could make with my hands. Oh give me something to *do*!

Our parents were involved and active enough in the life of the district. They both taught in the local primary school. As well as

being head teacher, my father led the Sunday school and sometimes preached on Sundays. He was expected to lead or take part
in every local activity or organization. Like the parson, my parents
were at the disposal of the people around them who came for
help, for advice, or just to talk. They told of illness, hardship and
poverty. The men invariably turned to the subject of 'government', a vague covering term for anyone in authority. What was
'government' doing, they would question, about the problems
that stared at us and lived with us year after year – the bad roads,
the unemployment, the lack of water? We shared in their feeling
of frustration and powerlessness. My parents cared about these
things: about people and their problems, about poverty and sickness, ignorance and superstition, about social injustice and the
way the country was governed. We listened and absorbed what we
heard, and learnt to care too.

Huntly was our cowman; tall, lean, hard-faced, brown-skinned.
He had served in World War I and he often reminded us of this,
using the French words he had picked up then. Perhaps he suffered shell-shock, for he had a wild look in his eyes; he was given
to outbursts of violent anger and later he became a broken-down
man. But in his prime he had an air of command and even the
simple process of milking a cow he invested with the atmosphere
of a military manoeuvre, requiring strategy and concentration.

He was knowledgeable and we depended on him. He prescribed bush baths for fever; he 'drenched' the cows with medicine; he dressed the navel of the baby calves; he knew when the
calves were due: 'Dat cow gwine drap soon, Teach'!' He shortened
everyone's names: my father became 'Teach' for Teacher, my
mother 'Miss Dais', and the parson (rector) 'Rec'. He lived
happily with his common-law wife. He told us how she would
bring him food in the field and would sing with him as he worked.

The hurricane of 1948 changed life for Huntly. We watched
anxiously through the closed windows as the first gusts of wind
bowed the coconut trees. Later we sat tense and silent in the darkened drawing room while my father braced himself against the
double leaves of the front door which threatened to burst open
with the wind. Even the panes of glass seemed to curve inward

with each blast and the leaves that spattered them struck with the sound of metal. The maid foolishly leaving the house when the wind was high just saved her neck from a flying sheet of zinc.

When it was nearly over someone came panting and troubled to the back door. We bundled out to see, anxious at what we might hear, glad to have news from another human being, whoever he might be. It was Huntly. The storm had blown his house down and he and his wife had escaped just in time. His wife was sick; he had carried her to neighbours who were looking after her. He himself had come up from the ridge where he lived along the road to our house, over fallen trees and in driving rain, to tell us this.

I see him now, a tall man making the passage seem crowded and low, his clothes ragged and reddish brown all over with mud, his skin shining with rain. A strong man, shaking and broken with grief. My imagination filled in the details of that scene; the narrow ridge on which his house stood, the darkened gullies on either side, then the white-washed thatched hut heaving over, making nothing of the carefully tended interior that meant home and security to two people; the desperate dash for cover, Huntly's arms and legs taut and gleaming wet, the limp white-wrapped figure of his wife, moaning, in his strong brown arms. She was ill; surely she would die, exposed to the fierce wind and rain. We forgot our fear, consumed at that moment with concern for Huntly, and, as we stared at him, the slowly built-up habit of caring burned into our heart and brain. So far all our knowledge of loss and suffering was second-hand. Could we be immune for ever?

CHAPTER II

The elementary school at Harewood was a long, rectangular wooden building raised above the uneven ground on short concrete slabs, and on longer wooden stilts where the ground sloped away towards the gully. 'Under school' had its peculiar memorable character; the cool sandy contours where we played shop and whispered secrets, the grooved slopes smelling of urine, littered with goats' droppings, infested with chigoes; the dark narrow places where a desperate boy, heedless of dirt, would wriggle to escape his pursuers. The school steps ended in the roadway which was our playground, but few cars came that way. There the boys played 'chase' and marbles and spun tops and the girls sang their ring games: 'Jane and Louisa' came home to their 'beautiful garden' which was a circle of little girls, black and brown and mostly bare-footed, standing on the stony roadway.

'Recess-time' had no fixed length; it seemed to depend on my father's judgment. Sometimes we played on and on into the long hot afternoon and we almost ran out of games. But one game always ended the recess period: 'Nanny, nanny, 'tring you needle, lang, lang t'read', we sang in broadest dialect, and abruptly the school bell would ring. Tolerant as he was, even Daddy could not take that song. The dialect could be pleasing and attractive but this song was harsh and ugly.

> 'Hat needle bu'n t'read, lang lang t'read.
> A lickle bit a needle but a lang lang t'read.'

So we crowded back into the school building, one long undivided room with a platform at one end so that it was useful for local entertainments and meetings. My father sat at the other end under the attendance board which read, 'Accommodation 200, number on roll 300'; but attendance varied from fifteen or twenty on Fridays to 270 on Tuesdays.

In front of my father stretched his kingdom of boys and girls, mostly black, here and there a Chinese or East Indian face, and some fair faces of German origin. We sat five or six together on long wooden benches with desks, the classes each with its blackboard and teacher, arranged facing different directions to distinguish between them. Classes were taken out of doors as often as possible. We stood round our teacher under the mango trees by the road and one after another droned from the reading book which we used for a whole year. Bored, we played with the sand and stones on the roadway while each reader was heard in turn. Or we chanted tables in unison, sitting on the school steps. We wrote on slates which we cleaned with water or saliva and rubbed with the hibiscus flower, fanning them in the sun and crying: 'Dry slate, dry, a gi' you quatty ginger bread!'

My father loved children; the younger ones would often come round his desk at recess-time to talk to him rather than join the others at play. He ruled with benevolence, but his patience gave way occasionally and not surprisingly: it was hard to achieve anything with pupils who came to school erratically as many did, and who were dull, dull, dull, perhaps because they were hungry, perhaps because they were tired, having jobs to do at home and walking long distances to school, perhaps because home and school were so unlike each other and to them school seemed boring and irrelevant. It was hard to work day after day in the drab, overcrowded building, using voice and leather strap, a few books, a few pictures and charts, slates and exercise books and little else; hard to meet the requirements of inspectors and to battle with ignorant, angry parents. When children wandered out of place, my father would stride through the school, strap in hand, and little legs scampered out of the way and order was restored. There was one day when a mother came to question the punishment he gave her child with raised voice and angry words, and before the hushed school my father's exasperation burst out: 'You are not fit to raise puppy dogs.'

My father's gift was eloquence: he had an easy flow of language and the ability to hold our interest with vivid detail. He enjoyed teaching and he enjoyed what he taught. He could bring even

Dickens' England near to us. He read to us in the top class from *A Tale of Two Cities*; Jerry Cruncher and Aggerawater had the crustiness and peevishness of people we knew, and we could feel and smell the steaming towels at the drunken orgies of Carton and Stryver.

Our books and our poems were from England, often about England, often illustrated by English scenes and faces. We chanted stanzas of 'The Solitary Reaper' and were saddened by the fate of Lord Ullin's daughter:

> 'The waters wild, went o'er his child,
> And he was left lamenting.'

We also learnt Scripture verses by heart and memory 'gems' intended to inspire us, such as:

> 'Lives of great men all remind us
> We can make our lives sublime,
> And, departing, leave behind us
> Footprints on the sands of time.'

We studied the soils of our district, sewed hats from dried grass and watched beans germinate in a glass jar; we heard snippets from our own history: Columbus and his three ships – easy to remember because of the rhythm they made – 'The Pinta, the Nina and the Santa Maria'; the awesome story of the destruction of Port Royal, the buccaneers' city. But the focus of our loyalty was Britain, culminating yearly on Empire Day, when we stood round the Union Jack and sang 'Land of Hope and Glory'.

CHAPTER III

'Mama, how do babies come?' My sister and I were five years old and my mother was expecting another baby. She was ready for this question; she must have rehearsed the answer many times before she needed to use it. Carefully she said, 'Mother and father come together in a special way, and God gives the mother a little baby which grows inside her until it is time for it to come out.' Our next question she could not have anticipated: 'How do you know when it is going to happen? Suppose it comes when you are in the road?' But her training as a teacher stood Mama well. In answering she related the beginning of labour to our own experience of natural need: 'I will know when it is going to happen just as you know when ... .' We were satisfied.

Steadily as we grew up she held up before us the goal of marriage as desirable and good, a precious wonderful relationship. Too anxiously, we thought even then. But understandably so. At school, she knew we would hear a different story – of unions without marriage, one mother bearing children by several different fathers, domestic quarrels and violence, as well as distorted sexual details. She tackled this problem in two ways: by constraining us to tell her all we heard and by warning her classes as she taught them, not to pass on these stories to us, for 'my children tell me everything'. She succeeded in silencing them and in isolating us painfully. How often on the brink of a juicy revelation, my informant would draw back: 'But ah won' tell you, for you gwine tell you mada.' Sometimes I gave in and promised not to tell and I would hear the forbidden tale. Later in the darkness when my mother is with us at bedtime, I know she requires our confidences and conscience smarts: 'Mama, do we *have* to tell you *every-thing?*' Wisely she would understand and let it go for that time.

I owe my conscience largely to my mother, though it manifested itself in ways neither my father nor herself approved of. She formed my earliest and deepest impressions of what God was like.

God was all-knowing. It was easy to believe that. My mother seemed to scan my every thought; she watched us and supervised every moment of our time.

And God never overlooked a sin. Neither did my mother. When we went visiting we dreaded the journey home and the first moments alone with Mama, for there was the inevitable post-mortem. 'You know you shouldn't sit listening when older people talk. You should go outside and play', or 'What were you doing out there with Linda? Some rudeness. She is not a nice child!'

Long after childhood when I felt moved to pray, I would begin resignedly, 'Lord, what have I done now?' For, often, when Mama called, it was to rebuke us. In contrast, Daddy called us to share something special – a curious insect he had found, a funny story in a magazine. Later I learnt that God calls also to share delight and to express His love, not only to point out sin and evoke guilt.

At the same time Mama must not be blamed for the excesses of our conscience and our religiosity. She deplored the long moments we spent on our knees trying to get through to God. She herself spoke of praying willingly and of finding comfort in it. Like the Psalmist she talked with God as she lay awake in her bed. We kept from her our own painful struggles with prayer. Neither did we confide to our parents the scruples that drove us to return even a pin we borrowed. Had they known, they would have feared for our sanity. For our part we envied the balance and sanity of their lives.

Where then did we learn or inherit the scrupulosity, the obsessiveness? Perhaps somewhere my mother had a hand in it. We were scrupulous and obsessive because we took ourselves too seriously. We took ourselves seriously because Mama took the business of bringing us up very seriously indeed. There was nothing haphazard about it; she was not working it out as she went along. The design, the aims and methods, she had worked out long in advance. We were her precious daughters, carefully schooled and moulded as a work of art.

Perhaps, later, we fought against God because we feared that, like Mama, He would limit our freedom and possess us completely. But in finding Him eventually, we found the One who cared infinitely; who, though He was the 'God of the whole earth', cared for us as if there were no one else beside us. And we responded warmly, for Mama's love and caring had whet our appetites for His love and through her we had learnt to respond.

CHAPTER IV

'Happy day when de marnin' come!
Happy day! By de ribber of Jordan!'

The old-fashioned gramophone scratched round the record of
the revival song. My brother jigged irreverently to the syncopated
tune and we grinned in shamefaced support.

The record went on:

'Bright soul, ah mek you tu'n back
You say you going a heaven
Wid you' banner in you' han'
An' you come a ribber Jordan an' you tu'n back.'

Cookie appeared at the door, her large bloodshot eyes glaring
angrily in her black face.

'Miss Daisy', she addressed my mother, 'see your children making fun of my church, Mam. Please to make them turn it off,
Mam.' The fun ended. No need for our mother to voice her rebuke; we knew her stand on this. Cookie was an adult, older than
my mother. We were children. And Cookie was a married woman.
Moreover her husband was pastor of the local Church of God. But
Cookie was our servant. Here was a delicate relationship to be
handled delicately. By all means Cookie must be treated with
gravity and respect. My own conscience added its rebuke,
schooled as it was by our parents to avoid even the appearance of
irreverence – we were never to use real prayers in our games as
when putting dolls to bed, and we never placed other books in a
pile on top of the Bible!

Cookie herself was a rebuke with her sincerity, the jewel of her
inner life, though this was almost obscured by the externals. For
Cookie did not please the eye – spreading in bosom and hip, neither
over-clean nor over-neat in dress, socks rolled down over her ankles,
a toe showing through the burst leather of her worn-down shoes.

Cookie, harsh in voice and unattractive even in laughter. My child's heart withdrew from Cookie and what she represented.

I saw that there was good in Cookie and reality in her religion but the expression of it was ludicrous, and revolting to my taste. I knew that seeing the good I should receive it, but I turned from the expression of it and in turning I assumed that I rejected the good too because they seemed to be inseparable: if I could not have one, I would not have the other. And even as I knew I was rejecting it I feared to do so, for I knew my reasons for turning were, in Scriptural terms, 'of this vain world'. And though I condemned myself I could not help myself. 'The common people heard him gladly': my conscience brought back to me that verse from Scripture about Jesus and ruthlessly applied it to myself: 'Had *you* lived then you would have rejected Him and kept to the respectable religion of the priests and Pharisees.'

My sister and I grew up believing in God. Just as the life of the church was woven into the pattern of our life and activity, so belief in God was taken up and knitted into the fabric of our minds. I accepted God as I accepted my parents. He was part of the world as I knew it. He was there. He had always been there. I have never doubted His existence for more than a passing moment.

We lived near the Anglican church to which we belonged, but there were other churches in the district as well. The Church of God met in a thatched hut with a beaten earth floor and rough wooden benches. It was known as the 'Wash-foot' church because the members washed one another's feet. Their services lasted for hours and we could hear from our house the shouting of the preacher and the lusty rhythmic singing of the congregation who clapped their hands as they sang. I was attracted by the joyful freedom of their singing, but I preferred the length of our own services and the style of our preachers, and I turned over and over in my mind their emphasis on personal salvation.

The Seventh-day Adventists were materially more prosperous and more restrained than the Church of God but their worship had a similar lively quality. When they held their baptismal services for adults in the nearby stream, the procession of singing people dressed in starched, snowy-white clothes attracted some of our church members, who joined them for the day, if not more permanently. I was impressed by their zeal in trying to convert other people. I myself had no desire to speak of my religion to anyone. I hardly knew what I would offer them if I did try.

The man holding forth in argument on the country bus was a Seventh-day Adventist. He was giving a reasoned presentation of Scripture to show that the resurrection took place on a Saturday. He quoted one account of the resurrection which read that Mary Magdalene came to the sepulchre 'at dawn' and found it empty. The 'dawn', he said, was the beginning of the day, but the day began on the evening of the previous day, for did we not read in Genesis that the evening and the morning were the first day? Evening and morning, in that order. Therefore when Mary Magdalene went to the tomb 'at dawn', it was not Sunday morning but Saturday evening.

No-one challenged him. His listeners did not know what to think. In the Anglican church we were taught that we kept the first day of the week in celebration of the resurrection. The Adventist was not to be outdone; his church also kept resurrection day, the *true* resurrection day, which was Saturday. The other churches, he continued, were mistaken. Worse than mistaken, they had been wilfully deceived by their parson. 'You see dem parson', he added, 'dem collar turn backways, dem is eddicated, dem know dem can fool you – dem t'row anyt'ing gie you!' No wonder our parson openly denounced them for heresy and sheep-stealing.

The Anglican church at Harewood had been there before the others. It stood on the ruins of an older, brick-built church destroyed in the earthquake of 1907. The oldest tombstone that still remains is dated 1852. In those days of larger properties of land, the surrounding people of quality, we were told, came to Harewood church. We could imagine them being jolted over the bumpy, dirt roads in horse-drawn carriages, the men in top hats and tails, the ladies wearing voluminous skirts bolstered by many petticoats, and beribboned bonnets. They would be English. The tombstones tell of Deborah and Gerald Waddington of Suffolk, England; of George Geddes, member of the Legislative Assembly, who also buried there, 'in grateful recollection' of 'honest worth and ever active zeal', his faithful servants 'William Stokes, a native of London' and 'Elizabeth Burdon, a native of Gloucester, England'.

Times changed, but not the sense of social pre-eminence in our church. Most of our congregation were poor and humble enough. This was particularly true on low Sundays. 'Barefoot Sundays', they were called. Then the parson was away, my father or another layman took the service, and the congregation consisted of a sprinkling of the old and poor, and, in the front benches, a number of barefooted boys who had stayed on from Sunday school.

In contrast, on special Sundays the church was filled with people. They came from miles around; their motor-cars lined the roadway. The front benches were packed with adults: the men perspiring over white shirt collars and dark heavy suits, the ladies fluttering fans to ease the discomfort of corsets and stockings and too-tight shoes, their hats and dresses smart and new. The church would be decorated with flowers and shrubs in special abundance and the choir would 'render an anthem', the invariable phrase of the announcing clergyman. It was a social occasion and the pleasures of looking and listening and the pride of belonging competed in my mind with the religious significance of the day.

Church services were long and distractions were welcome; the roving lizard that sent the organist from her stool; the pelting rain that cooled and darkened the church; the parson's son in the front row overcome with giggles. When these failed, I tried to listen and find meaning in what was going on. I soon knew many of the canticles and prayers by heart and became familiar with passages of the Bible.

Together with this slow, steady process of absorbing the teaching of the church came the occasional stabs of discomfort and unease. I heard of hell and heaven; without doubt I preferred to be heading for the latter, but I was not sure that I was. There seemed to be a dividing line between 'the child of God' and 'the child of the world', the 'sheep and the goats', the 'saved and the unsaved', which had nothing to do with forms of baptism and confirmation, church attendance and saying of prayers. It had something to do with the 'heart' and not with outward ritual.

Every year we heard the lesson read where the words oc-
curred, 'You must be born again'; and the doubt revived, the
doubt about my own position. I heard of the courage and zeal of
the first apostles and realized I knew nothing of this. I would try
as a child to lull myself into a sense of security by saying, 'I am
all right; my family are all right. We know the parson. We are his
friends. He visits us and sits on our verandah and has long talks
with my father. We are on the right side.' But this did not stand
up to the test of death.

I knew even then that in death I would be alone; I could not
take the parson with me, or my parents. The lonely part of me
that was myself, separate from other selves, would stand before
God. Credentials of baptism and churchgoing would sound hol-
low then. This alone would matter: that in my inner, lonely,
naked self I was a friend of God. But was I a friend of God? I did
not want to be a friend of God. Certainly I did not give form to
these thoughts in childhood but I knew them in some symbolic
way, and every other childish fear and unhappiness was nothing
to the awfulness of that knowledge. I escaped it if I could,
but I did not want to erase it altogether. It seemed supremely
important to keep it alive.

Occasionally I put God to the test, not in cold blood, but when
I was afraid of the dark, of hurricane or of earthquake. Could He
put away my fear? Would He? Did we not learn to sing:

> 'You need not fear the storm or the earthquake shock,
> You're safe for evermore if you build on the Rock'?

Once, after a frightening series of earthquakes, I had a vivid
dream of the head of Christ, as I had seen it drawn in Bible illus-
trations, standing out against the darkness of the gloomiest
wooded corner we could see from our verandah at night. My heart
was drawn to Him and I wrote pages of little verses in my ruled
exercise book to express my love and gratitude to Him.

This stage passed. The fears remained. God did not give peace
as I expected. He did not banish the feelings of terror and panic at
the moment when I prayed. I stopped asking and became a little
hardened against God. But this experience was good. I rejected

the idea that God would play the part of an indulgent mother, taking the sting out of every unpleasant event for my sake. But the question remained open. God loved me! How else would He show that love, if He did not deliver me from real suffering when I asked Him?

CHAPTER V

Early in our lives skin colour took on meaning for us. My father might have passed for white in England, though not in Jamaica. My mother's skin was smooth chocolate. My sister and I were in between them in colouring, and my brother was like my mother. We had relatives of every shade from black to white. Colour- and shade-consciousness was a family affliction. We learnt early that to be white was very desirable and to be black a misfortune. My mother considered it a feather in her cap that she had married a 'good brown man' and not someone darker or of the same colouring as herself, rather as another woman might applaud herself on managing to catch a rich husband. My father was more sophisticated; he remained aloof from considerations of colour, though we suspected his vanity was touched by my mother's reverent regard for the colour of his skin.

We had no doubt whatever that my mother expected us to choose a husband who was at least the same colouring as ourselves, if not lighter. To marry and produce children of lighter colour than oneself was to 'raise' the colour of the family. To raise the colour of the family was to raise its social status. All around me there was evidence that colour and class were linked: black people were mostly poor and uneducated, the people of property and social and professional standing were mostly white or light-skinned. There were many exceptions, but this was the general trend.

This is not surprising. The belief that the black-skinned man was at a disadvantage is no fiction of the Jamaican mentality; it is a fact of our history, perhaps too well known to bear repetition. The black man came to Jamaica as a slave imported from Africa. He was removed from his tribal setting with its social organization, its standards and values; he lost his language. After the abolition of slavery most slaves left their masters, to eke out an existence on land that in many cases was hardly fit for cultivation; little or no provision was made for education. Beside him the white slave-owner and his children, both white and coloured, lived in striking contrast having advantages of wealth and property, education, training in an established cultural pattern, and access to positions of responsibility and leadership. Therefore, broadly speaking, the white and coloured Jamaicans had a head start over the black in the early days after slavery.

It was out of this historical situation that the attitude and prejudices developed which I absorbed from members of my own family and people around me generally. The term 'black' was more than a label of social class; it was used to imply degradation of character, a person altogether undesirable. The black forbears of my mother's family were spoken of regretfully and as if they belonged to a dim distant past. These black forbears accounted for relatives who were 'turned down', that is, who did not succeed socially and materially and seemed to have no desire to do so; they were to be blamed for the stubborn, kinky hair that one child in a family would have among a number of soft, wavy-haired sisters.

In my mother's family the black ancestor could not be disowned because his marks were obvious among them. But in my father's family, which had a great proportion of white forbears, he was never mentioned; we turned our backs resolutely against him. There was a pencilled drawing of my great-grandparents on my father's side which was passed round the family. Great-grandfather wore a moustache and a stiff white collar; great-grandmother had long pliant hair plaited round her head and, it was pointed out, a riding habit, a mark of her social status. He was part Scottish, she was part Jewish, we were told. What the other part of their racial inheritance was, was never mentioned. It was without doubt African, Negro, slave, black – unspeakable.

'Black faces, black faces everywhere, and more black faces than brown. Pass over the black faces. Greet the brown face! Ah, a white face! Gaze on it with pleasure and admiration!'

This was the burden of the attitude that I adopted, and so I disintegrated myself. For, being brown face, I was both black and white face in one, and more black face than white. I could not change my brown face, but I was pleased only with a white face and I wanted to forget the black faces altogether. Here was the seed of trouble.

CHAPTER VI

My mother had clear ideas on the moral standards she wanted her children to have and the social status she wanted us to achieve. Her family came from the savannahs of St Elizabeth, physically sturdy, hard-working, ambitious and proud of their allegedly Scottish descent. One of her great-uncles, she would often say, was a Presbyterian lay preacher with the added distinction of a long white beard.

Her chief fear was for our chastity. It was implicit in our up-bringing that we would not identify ourselves with the majority of people round us who lived in concubinage and among whom pregnancy outside a stable relationship was common. But she often told us of the daughter of a middle-class family who had been seduced by the yard-boy. This cautionary tale impressed upon us that it could happen even to us, but here we felt she went too far. This was the measure of my mother's success in shaping our attitudes, that we thought it unnecessary and insulting to have this story brought to our notice.

It was also our mother's aim that we should speak correctly in English: 'You spoke so nicely when you were five or six', she would lament, but after a few years in the primary school we were proficient in the dialect spoken by all our companions. This was to speak 'badly'.

As both our parents taught in the school, my mother was able to keep her watchful eye on us for most of her waking hours. In her anxiety to shield us from stories of immorality and frightening accounts of death or witchcraft told by other children in school, she would banish us from time to time to the Teacher's Cottage where we would stand and watch our companions shout and run in free-dom on the other side of the fence. Somewhere, we longed, there would be children with whom we could identify ourselves com-pletely – children whose parents had the same values as our own, who spoke in English and not in dialect, whose activities and conversation we could take part in without guilt or misgiving, knowing it was with Mama's full blessing. It was with this hope that we looked forward to secondary school.

My mother set her heart on sending my sister and myself to St Hilary's, a boarding school for girls in Market Town some fifty miles from Harewood. It was going to be difficult for them to afford to send two children to boarding school, but they had arranged for us to sit for government scholarships and, with characteristic faith, they obtained places for us at the school and prepared our uniforms before knowing the result of the examination. Their faith was rewarded; my sister won a full scholarship covering all her expenses and later I too was awarded a similar one.

The school was exactly as my mother wanted it to be – a community where we were well protected physically and morally and where we received a sound academic education as well as training in social graces.

My sister and I wept noisily as the school bus set out taking us to St Hilary's for the first time. Surrounding us was a sea of girls in crisp clean cotton uniforms and wide-brimmed straw hats, buttressed with hockey sticks and tennis racquets. The informality and the quietness of home, the privacy and the leisure, were behind us.

That awful school bus. It sauntered, it laboured up Mount Diablo, it ambled over the stony portions of the road leading into Market Town, in noonday heat, through craggy mountain country, monotonously wooded, where the undisturbed wisps of grey-green old man's beard trailed down from the dark-leaved pimento trees.

Six hours. We had our lunch with us and ate it as we went. No-one left the bus for any reason. Except on this first occasion. One girl was taken out by the mistress in charge. She was a new girl, so new that she wore a pretty embroidered linen dress instead of the blue and white school uniform, and her hair flowed round her shoulders. She was crying. Why are you crying? The bus was stopped. She was interrogated in privacy outside. Her need was simple and natural enough but there was no provision for this along the way. Ordinary people took to the bush, but St Hilary's never descended to the expedients of ordinary people. The journey was resumed.

We arrived at the school, passing at last through the gates, up the long driveway to the top of the hill and onto the grey, paved courtyard, a flagpole at its centre. The building, E-shaped, rose up round the courtyard, pale stone at its base, wooden beams and plaster at the upper floors in imitation Tudor. Three pointed towers on the shingled roof looked down across the playing fields and the town in the valley to the western hills, fold after fold growing paler in the distance. Above them the sunset would flash magnificent red and orange in the evening sky. Spathodia and poinciana trees near the courtyard and playing fields were in bloom at times in the year; tall, leafy, rounded trees, shining green, rose up straight against the seaside blue of the sky; the air was crisp and sparkling bright, and cool even in summer. These things I loved.

Above the stone pillars of the entrance, Latin inscriptions were cut, and in the wooden archway of the inner porch the lines from the Psalms: 'Except the Lord build the house, they labour in vain that build it.' Piety, the love of natural beauty and of high and lofty things were here. Those who founded the school loved these things, as our school hymn, composed by a former headmistress, frequently reminded us:

> 'Here in our hillside school we feel Thy presence.
> By starlight, dawn and sunset Thou art near.
> Oh may Thy earthly glory lead us heavenward,
> Our shining eyes lit up by vision clear.'

We recognized and loved these things also. We settled well into boarding school life. We liked the order and security, we were always occupied and, for the first time, fully stretched mentally.

CHAPTER VII

St Hilary's had high standards, high moral standards, high standards of social behaviour. We learned to believe in these standards, to accept them as the best, to live by them and to pass them on without compromise. I gave my unquestioning loyalty to St Hilary's. This was what I wanted – to belong, to be identified, to be approved, and St Hilary's filled that need.

This did not mean that I found friends. Here I was disappointed. I had expected to meet many girls exactly like myself. I was surprised to find that this was not so. There were people even here who did things which my mother would not have approved of! Not everyone wanted to accept authority as I wanted to, and the most popular set in my form lived, so they said, a gay, unrestricted life at home, which was unheard of in mine. They presented to my credulous eyes a uniform picture of themselves made up and clad in scanty shorts, reclining on cushions, munching chocolates and listening to the radio, with perhaps a boyfriend hovering by. I did not qualify. Once again I was isolated, different, as I was when I was forbidden to play with other children at home.

Here at St Hilary's, as at Harewood, I did well at school work, better than most people. This increased my isolation. I worked hard to maintain my superior position. If I could not be popular, at least I would have prestige. Social prestige was out of the question; socially and materially most girls were better off than I.

As with my age-group, so with those in authority, whose rules I sought so loyally to keep and whose tasks I worked at so diligently, I formed no satisfactory relationship. Is this ever possible? Can a phalanx of fluctuating adults ever supply the longing for close, constant belonging of a child dislodged from home? Perhaps at twelve I should have been ready for this casting from the womb, but I was not.

The beginning was painful; blow after blow came, like jagged thrusts on naked, undefended flesh. They began with the school bus and the cruel indifference to urgent physical need. Then the first cold shower at 6.30 in the morning. We followed the other girls down a maze of passages and stairways to the cold stone basement, past the supervising mistress sitting by her register of names – 'Good morning, Miss James' – into the dimness before a line of cells. I went into one and looked from the straw-seated chair and the pegs by the door to the wooden slatted footstool and up to the rough metal shower disc with two pathetic pieces of string on either side of it. Cold grey concrete walls, whitewashed concrete ceiling.

How did one have a bath here? I wanted to run away. I stepped out again into the passage and near to tears I looked round for someone to whom I could appeal. But what would I say? How to admit that I had never used a bath like this before? Better to keep this to myself. I learnt in time to cope with the ordeal of the cold shower, to avoid the first piercing trickle of water, to race through and out and up from the dungeon, tingling and relieved into the sunshine and freshness of the new day. But this came later.

That morning there were other hurts to come. I was still thirsty after my cup of cocoa. 'May I have some milk?' I asked, and was answered with this cold rebuff: 'Are you paying for extra milk?' Eight pairs of eyes looked at me as the message was passed down to me from mouth to mouth. Too many eyes for tears. Fight to hold back the tears.

After breakfast I wandered off on my own for what seemed a very short time and when I returned to the classroom, my mind misted with pain and ignorance of what was happening round me, I found the others standing smartly by their desks waiting for the first lesson to begin. My sister glared tensely. 'Where were you?' she bit out at me. I had missed form-room time, roll call and prayers in the Hall. All in what seemed no time at all. So I was introduced to the relentless pace of the timetable, and to the hurt was added the strain of keeping up the pace – the hysterical fear of being left behind. To avenge myself for the hurts I had received, I became difficult in class, insisting at times on exact and detailed explanations, refusing to use my own understanding. If any mistress took notice of the 'exasperating twins' (for my sister reacted in the same way) she either ignored our behaviour or misinterpreted it, determining that 'the twins must be squashed'.

Only one person seemed to see the need and the pain behind it and with her gracious manners soothed and healed me. Not only did Miss Ealing give me the support I needed, but in her I found someone I wanted to copy, for she combined in herself qualities which I wanted to see together but which, from my experience of other people, seemed necessarily incompatible. Let me explain.

Just as we learnt 'what the school stood for', so we also came to see that the mistresses varied in their commitment to these values. There were the 'pillars' of the school, mostly the people who stayed for years and old girls who came back to teach for shorter periods. And there were the rest of the staff; the neutral, the indifferent and the objecting. The subtle judgment as to where each person stood began among the staff themselves and seeped down among the girls; never explicitly, for girls were discouraged from discussing the staff and it was unthinkable that one mistress would discuss another with a girl.

From what I absorbed and observed I built up my own stereotype of what the ideal 'pillar' of St Hilary's should be like and I set out to fashion myself and my judgment of others by it. It was a true stereotype, in that it was drawn from a few and was neglectful of the complexities and contradictions in the people from whom it was drawn. It came partly from the first headmistress I knew, Miss Tell; tall, erect, unbending, invariably dressed in a cotton shirt frock, her long dark-brown hair drawn back in a bun, with some fullness and undulation round the forehead to relieve the severity of her appearance. 'It is vanity', she was reported to have said, 'to keep changing one's hair style.'

Like her, my ideal St Hilary's mistress had stage presence; she was taken from Shakespeare, Molière, the British navy – commanding, eloquent. She kept her distance with inferiors. She was isolated socially and the school was all her world. To be feminine was frivolous; for a mistress to be warm and companionable to the girls was to cheapen herself and to undermine authority; not to be able to hold forth dramatically was to be weak and ineffective. In my child's mind it was either ... or. Either this sterile, aloof, histrionic being which was the ideal, or the more rounded, human person who was to be rejected.

Miss Ealing shattered this distinction. She was both … and. She came after I had been at school for more than a year and at once identified herself with the establishment. But she was human as well as high principled. She bent to touch the child she spoke to, and spoke gently and courteously; yet she was well able to command the attention of many. She could deal wounds faithfully and lovingly; she was without sentimentality, yet not cold.

But here again there could be no satisfying relationship. She did not belong to me, I did not belong to her and only an exclusive relationship could satisfy. Besides, she was not always there. Her supporting presence went in and out like the English sun in April or October, and therefore I sustained myself on unreal imaginings.

Of the rest of the staff, one other mistress stands out. Miss Hobbs also made a lasting and deeply-incised effect on me. She baffled, disturbed and overwhelmed me; her personality engulfed mine. She was impressive and she could not be ignored. She spoke fluently and with force, and she stood for impressive things – honour, loyalty, service, the sacrificing of the individual to principle. She was also a good actress and enjoyed a little her power to over-awe and compel. Miss Hobbs had the trappings of command – broad-shouldered height, flashing eyes, the sneering lip, expressive hands. Her rulings ranged widely: about work, which was to be done to perfection and given in on time (we strained every brain cell and still were found lacking); about correct posture and diction, the careful phrasing of requests and observations (she could read insolence in the merest turn of the shoulder and disposition of the hands); about clothes-sense and social behaviour – for example, how tactfully to distract a persistent partner at a dance.

I also have kinder memories of her. When at fifteen I fell in love I confided in her. He was a theological student, and already in adolescent confidence I looked forward to my role as a parson's wife. She was silent. With adult pessimism she could see the disappointment that might lie ahead but she kept back the shocked 'Oh no!' Instead she spoke gently and positively, describing what it could be like to be a parson's wife – the sacrifices of near poverty, the need to be withdrawn and prayerful.

CHAPTER VIII

Any resemblance between St Hilary's and an English girls' boarding school was far from accidental. The school had probably been founded with the English expatriate in mind. The girls were being prepared for further education in an English university, or life in an Anglicized community. The headmistress was English and so were many of the staff, and some of the Jamaican staff had been trained in England.

The curriculum was imported from England; the books and subject-matter were English. Even the exercise books were sent from Foyles in London. This only continued what had begun at Harewood, for at that time, even in the elementary school, we learnt to read from books prepared for English schools, illustrated with pictures of rolling English wheat-fields and well-clad English children climbing over stiles. In our more advanced readers we met reproductions of the English painters, Turner and Constable, whose muted colours seemed incredible to our eyes which were so well used to vivid sunshine, contrast of light and shade, and brilliant colours.

Also from England were the spoken accents, the niceties of behaviour and, in spite of the difference in climate, the uniform. When my sister and I began our internment there in 1943, the serge skirts had just been replaced by blue cotton tunics, but some seniors were still wearing black stockings.

I use 'internment' deliberately. The life of the school, especially for the boarders, was cut off from the town, and indeed from everything around it – from the social and cultural mixture of Jamaican life, and from communications with the outside world. We did not read the papers unless we were in the top forms, but perhaps we lost little; the day of the transistor radio was not yet and the school radio set was rarely used. We did not speak to the maids; we did not ask the daygirls to bring or buy anything for us. We wrote letters once a week. These could be written to parents, to a brother or to female friends and relatives but to no-one else without specific permission, and the addressed envelopes were checked.

Every Sunday we sallied forth as a school to go to the local Anglican church. For this weekly contact with the outside world we walked in crocodile wearing white dresses and wide Panama hats, flanked by members of staff. We filed into church, sat in a block by ourselves, and filed out afterwards without a word to our fellow churchgoers.

Occasionally we were taken to a film at the local cinema. At first we took our place with the rest of the world, but on one occasion there was an epidemic in the town; the head and staff of the school hesitated about exposing the girls to infection in a shared cinema. The cinema was fumigated, the school sat at a private showing in exclusive possession of the building, and thereafter it was always arranged we had the cinema to ourselves when we saw a film. On our walks and our visits to the local shops we were always attended by at least a prefect or someone in authority, and we could walk about the grounds only in those places where we were unlikely to meet the servants or the local people without being in sight of a member of staff.

The dialect had no place here. This was what I looked forward to and what my parents wanted; but when it came I had a sense of loss. For twelve years of my life almost everyone around me spoke the dialect, and I spoke it well myself. At school we had no contact with such people. I had to shut away the memories of Harewood – the gay children calling in the playground of the primary school or shouting at the river where they came to fetch water, the maids laughing and telling Anancy* stories, the workmen singing as they dug up the railway sleepers, the butcher's musical call at the bend of the road as he brought the mutton. These people and others like them came and went from my home in Harewood daily. Now I was cut off from them and I missed their voices. I found I had to learn a new language. The language of St Hilary's was different from the English I had used at home or heard in church or met in

---

* Anancy is a spider, the hero of Jamaican folk lore, originating in West Africa.

books. It was not even like the more sophisticated speech of friends and cousins who lived in Kingston. The choice of words, the cadences were different. Our first headmistress, Miss Tell, was English and a graduate of Oxford University; at first I found her completely unintelligible!

It was one thing to find to my surprise that the English I had used before was different. But more than this, I also came to regard it as unacceptable, and this was painful. Scrupulously and sometimes unjustifiably I set to work to suppress the familiar phrases and pronunciation and to replace them with the new. As with every other standard that St Hilary's upheld, I accepted this as the language that ought to be used at all times everywhere, and if I modified it at any time, even in the holidays – let alone at school – I would feel guilty.

But out of school we were forced to modify our speech: 'People in Jamaica don't say *payriod* and *searious* the way you do', one of our friends at Harewood remarked. 'That is affected. We say *pee-riod* and *seerious*.' He was kinder than most, for he spoke openly to us and with concern rather than ridicule. Others were silent and seemed to withdraw from us in resentment against our newly acquired affectation. They resented not only our speech but what seemed to them our stilted and exaggerated mannerisms as well. But in spite of the pain of isolation and conflict that I experienced then, I cannot entirely regret this legacy of speech and manners from St Hilary's, for when I came to England I found acceptance and ease in social contacts, no doubt because of them.

At St Hilary's we studied the literature of England and later of France; we graduated from 'Lord Ullin's Daughter' to the poetry of Wordsworth, Keats and Shelley, and to our study of English history was added the marriage intrigues and war-mongering of the European dynasties.

The younger children were taught the geography of Jamaica, but as I entered school at twelve I bypassed these earlier forms, and though our English science books described the frogs and morning glory which we knew, they left out the lizard and the mongoose, the hibiscus and the ackee – the wealth of plant life, birds and animals that were all around us. Our syllabus was determined by the external examinations of Cambridge University and our examination papers were sent all the way to England to be marked. Therefore, since my mind and imagination were fed on English scenes and English thoughts, it became imperative for me to go to England, to bring to fulfilment these experiences which were begun at school.

But things Jamaican could not be excluded altogether. 'No arguing in here. Out of the form room, if you are going to argue about politics!' We were fourteen-year-olds and our form captain was repeating what she said almost daily, to keep the required level of peace and order in the form room. We were arguing about politics, Jamaican politics, and two of the leading parties in Jamaica were supported fiercely by rival groups in our form. For it was about 1945 and Jamaica had just achieved universal suffrage, full representation and a measure of self-government. St Hilary's had opened its shutters a little to let in the wind of national feeling, and we had just staged a mock election. While the Second World War lasted we followed its progress drearily in our civics classes. Now our attention was directed to our own country and we were actively taking part in the political life that was surging round us.

But our response alarmed our teachers. This response came almost entirely from our form. It was the largest in the school, numbering thirty, and in it were a high proportion of girls on scholarships and others of wholly Jamaican background, whose increasing numbers would gradually change the character of the school. In this form there were others like myself whose parents were involved and active in the new political life, and the school's mock election encouraged our interest and enthusiasm. To the dismay of the staff, we argued and stormed at each other for months after this event. They never allowed this to happen again. They did not take the opportunity to use our interest and enthusiasm to explore and learn and think about our country. If they did try, I have forgotten, for I have no memories of civics classes after that.

Our national feeling found another outlet and we began to put on plays and entertainments in the local dialect. Though many girls abstained from taking part, and a few objected, we found that most people in the school enjoyed these entertainments and the idea spread to other forms. We were aggressively Jamaican, and so we were a threat to the Anglicized atmosphere of the school. By our greater numbers and by our outlook we threatened the discipline and the traditions of the school. The staff reacted by an increase of rules, a tightening up of controls. They did not begin then to question the school's existing aims and values; they prepared to defend these values to the last.

This battle was inevitable since in the school were mirrored the changes taking place outside it – in politics, where the barely-grown David was taking aim at the colonial giant, and in social values where the new cultural wine surged against the old. In myself at least, then and now, the new and the old wine flow side by side and David and Goliath are Siamese twins, not fighting now but still not reconciled.

For me there are new battles, but having begun early I developed a taste for fighting and I like to fight still.

CHAPTER IX

The moral climate of St Hilary's was severe. For thoroughness and watchfulness and seeing that rules were kept the school could hardly have been bettered. It might have seemed a simple thing to break the rules, but in fact they were kept by the majority most of the time. I do not know how many rules there were and now I would not try to guess. I never counted them though I heard them often enough. Term after term, year after year they were read out in the Hall before the assembled school in a long, indigestible stream with 'suggestions for behaviour' tacked on at the end.

On my first Sunday at school I wrote home to say that there were one hundred rules. As I was a new girl, my letter was read by the presiding mistress who asked me to write it again; 'one hundred' was untrue. She did not say how many rules there were; perhaps there were fifty or even only twenty-five but in my eyes there were 'one hundred rules', 'too many rules', and this I knew my parents would understand.

Every moment of the day and even the night was covered by rules. I knew when I came in by the lobby at the entrance that I must keep silence, I must remember to consult the notice board, I must not run, I might go straight on or turn left, but not turn right, as that took me past the headmistress's study – except when it rained, then I might turn right. If I forgot something upstairs I must find the mistress on duty and get her permission to go for it; once there, I might not speak and run on the verandahs, I might not go into any other dormitory but my own, and if I passed through another dormitory on my way to my own I might not loiter or speak to anyone there. And so on, all through the day, even at weekends and even if I woke at night.

We went to bed, woke, dressed, ate, worked and played to the bang of a bell. There was only one choice to be made – the moral choice, whether to obey or defy authority. Every moment was mapped out, every role and duty well defined not only during the working week but also at weekends. At half term the rules were not relaxed for those who stayed at school, but only then did we have long periods of time free of prescribed activity.

No wonder when I emerged from school ('With days set free to learn and test our powers', ran the hymn), I was like some woodland creature accustomed to living underground, unhappy and unsure in the light and freedom. Yet every one of these restrictions could be justified; I myself have, on occasion, vigorously supported them. How can many live and work together smoothly without some loss of freedom? But could it have been less severe?

The loss of freedom we suffered at St Hilary's was so severe because the rules were made not just for our protection, but also to protect the good name of the school. We were being protected from physical injury ('no running is allowed, nor climbing trees'), and from moral contamination (we were forbidden even to hold hands) not only for our own sakes, but also that no parent or outside authority could accuse the school, 'You let them … what did you expect?' And while some outsiders may thus have forced the school into restrictiveness, others like my own parents were too acquiescent. They were too content with the school's restrictions, for they were able to sleep comfortably while we were at St Hilary's, knowing that their daughters were safer there than they themselves could keep them at home.

But such restrictiveness was not altogether for our good. I, for one, did not need so much to be restrained as to learn to use freedom. I needed to be thrust out, to exercise judgment and, within limits, to take the consequences of making my own choices. For I responded to the rules by being completely subject to them. I made myself comfortable in the security of being told exactly what to do and I was pleased to abdicate responsibility for my actions.

'May I leave what's on my plate?' I asked one day at table. It was one miserable piece of yam, but we were not allowed to leave anything without permission. The exasperated head girl at the top of the table, weary of running other people's lives, retorted, 'What do you think? I leave you to decide.'

I ate the yam, as she must have known I would, mortified that I did not dare to leave it, annoyed and surprised at having the decision cast back at me, for, having a very tender conscience, I saw the matter of eating a piece of yam as one of moral consequence. This was not due entirely to my tender conscience, however. The spirit in which the rules were enforced by the dominant personalities of the school encouraged this fallacious interpretation. The examples could be multiplied. If I walked past a piece of paper lying on the floor and did not pick it up I would feel guilty, for if I were seen to do this I could be reprimanded, not tolerantly, humorously, acknowledging the triviality of the offence, but fiercely and sternly as if it were a grave misdemeanour.

I suffered constantly: there were so many things I might do which were wrong. If only I could drift into forgetfulness sometimes! But my wretchedly good memory and tender conscience kept me conscious every moment of what the school decreed I should be doing then. Usually my obedience was rewarded, if not by approbation, at least by being left in peace. But sometimes it increased my suffering. The school decreed that every illness must be reported to the nurse. But Nurse, in self-protection, ensured against malingering by meeting these reports with suspicion and voiced exasperation. For me, a slight headache or a cold beginning meant torment – either the harrowings of conscience if I did not report it (was there not a risk of more serious illness?) or the loud hostility of Nurse.

I became a prefect, and to the burden of keeping the rules myself was added the responsibility of seeing that others kept them. I was not popular, for I applied to the younger girls the scrupulous standards I inflicted on myself. A commonly broken rule was that of silence in the lobby by the notice board. At times, if I knew that girls were there, I would avoid the lobby, taking a long route through the building rather than face the strain of having to rebuke them. This was no real escape, for my self-esteem was damaged. I suffer still. The feelings of self-condemnation to which I am subject by nature were so reinforced by these years of moral tyranny at St Hilary's that they prevail even in adulthood. I may be forgiven if I want to bruise the tyrant a little.

CHAPTER X

It was afternoon and gentle sunshine. Lessons were over. Everything enticed one to exuberance, but around the school there was oppressive, noonday silence. By Miss Tell's command we must all move quietly and not speak because, at the top of the building in the sick-room, supervised by Miss Tell herself, a solitary junior mistress, an old girl of the school, was sitting a scholarship examination for Oxford University. I was a new girl then and the awesome passage of that hushed afternoon impressed on me a reverence for academic excellence which was next only to religious piety.

That junior mistress did gain entrance to Oxford University and the school rejoiced with a half-holiday. Here was the strength of St Hilary's, that it provided the perfect setting for academic work. Nothing was allowed to disturb our periods of study. But the measured order extended to all areas of our life in the school, and in this lay the weakness of St Hilary's, for it failed to prepare us for the topsy-turvy nature of life in the very different world outside.

There was no muddle. My person and belongings were sacred, inviolable. No small brother meddled with my possessions, used my towels, mislaid my pencils, attacked me in a tantrum. No muddle. And no huddle. I was free from the annoyances (and the warmth) of living constantly in a close emotional relationship. No hovering parent heard and saw too much. I belonged to myself, self-centred and unruffled. Occasionally there was some huddle and muddle, as in the controlled disorder back-stage of our plays and entertainments. I exulted in this, but only briefly, and I was afterwards only too pleased to help restore all the placid order again.

There was, moreover, at least one sphere in which the order and placidity were challenged. This was in the Girl Guides and, though I joined, I resisted its challenge, especially in camping. Camping meant roughing it, meant that people and possessions were thrown together with no special areas prescribed or proscribed. I was not told exactly what to do. The cooking, for example, had to be worked out as we went along and, worse, together with other people.

Here was huddle, muddle, fun, freedom, exploration; and I turned weakly and cowardly away.

My bookish habits, however, had unlimited reinforcement. There were games every afternoon; singing, dancing, gym and music lessons were part of the timetable. But the chief occupation of the day given most time and weight was sitting before a book. Yet I developed no taste for exploration – the bear-like activity of going over the mountain to see what I could see. I settled comfortably into the habit of absorbing canned information, sorting, analysing, storing it and giving it back intact, but never going beyond it.

What there was in me of daring and inventiveness had died in my first term. For my first essay I wrote about the sea enthusiastically, beginning with a stream of adjectives that filled three lines. It was returned with a line – disdainful, red – drawn obliquely through my supreme effort. After that I kept to the prosaic. Not again would I expose my imagination to that cruel pen. I gave up my private opinion and all confidence in my own judgment. I gained much that was good, undoubtedly, for I had good teachers; but I also lost something very important.

One exceptional girl in my sixth-form years challenged this. One evening, as we walked upstairs to bed she commented, 'They say there are three men in your life – your first love, your true love, and the man you marry. I hope I shall find all three in one.' Her remark burst like a comet on the tameness of my mental horizon. She had taken a given statement, challenged it and reshaped it by her own thinking. My feelings were a mixture of wonder at her greater maturity of thought, jealousy that she had arrived there before I had, and pleasure that I also could explore such thinking.

Dotted through the day and week there were a few domestic activities – some sewing classes, bed-making, mending, shoe-cleaning. But the school was not equipped for teaching cooking and other household skills, and one attempt to send us to a neighbouring school for this was soon given up. I was content. Drudgery was not for me. Let someone else empty the slops, take away the offending laundry, stack and clear and wash the dirty dishes ('soul-destroying work' as Miss Hobbs once described it, shuddering). The thought that I would ever live in a servant-less society and wake day after day to these tasks and little else never disturbed my serenity. I looked forward to a life in adulthood as near as possible to life as we lived it at home and at St Hilary's. When I came to marriage and mother-hood I was unprepared, bewildered.

There was a want of social charity at the school that went ill with the profession of Christian piety. The girl who threw her prepara-tion book on the floor in disappointment at the low mark given to her efforts was disgraced with, 'You vulgar fishwife!' A loud, un-covered sneeze was labelled a 'drayman's sneeze'. A senior mis-tress standing on the platform in the Hall before the gathered school and inveighing against some insolent or careless behaviour summed it up by saying, 'That is the sort of thing the maids do!' She could hardly have taken thought for the child among whose relatives there was a maid, and this might easily have been true among the girls on scholarships. Even American variations in table manners were deplored. 'That may be how it's done by our American friends ...', conceded Miss Hobbs, but with the word 'friends' went a sneer, and the variant custom was forbidden.

In these and other ways we were taught matters of custom with a rigidity that made adjustment to the manners of a different soci-ety seem morally wrong. The idea came subtly into my mind, and I accepted it, that certain forms of behaviour were to be avoided not so much because they were undesirable in themselves but be-cause they were done by people of low social position. And yet it is unquestionable that the staff were striving hard for what was good, but what was also, at times, trivial. While they struggled with the motes of pronunciation (we learnt to say 'gels' for 'girls' and 'wen' for 'one') and with the nice handling of the table napkin (not 'serviette', mind you), they bolstered the beams of self-righteous pride and social superiority.

I drank in the false ideas. I found it easy to believe that menial occupation and low social position were synonymous with vulgar-

ity, and hard to see that dignity is with the humblest, that simplicity can have grace, and that good manners are considerateness for
others and not a high veneer of ritual words and poses. St Hilary's
tried to say this too, but only grudgingly. Or was my eye jaun-
diced? Certainly my own superior attitude at this time could be
expressed in this way:

> 'I thank God I am not as other girls are;
> I am a St Hilary's girl,
> I use my fork alone for mince
> And the point of my spoon for porridge.
> I cry Hurra! I do not shout Hooray!
> I am a nice person; I am neither crude nor rude.
> Admire me, even if you cannot like me.'

It was an objectionable attitude. If I could wake and find it was a
dream that I was like this, I would be happy.

St Hilary's gave me awareness and taught me social skills. But I
did not learn till afterwards that I must become part of the varied
stream of life, with its ugliness and drudgery, that my hands must
be soiled and my body submit to gross labour. I? Not I. I am a
St Hilary's girl. Not all because of St Hilary's, however. For
these were lessons I was by nature not disposed to learn and the
seeds of my false attitudes were sown at Harewood, as I have
shown, long before I went to St Hilary's.

CHAPTER XI

St Hilary's carried on my religious education. It was a Church of England school. I felt at home. The spiritual pace was set by my first headmistress, Miss Tell. We were encouraged to use the school chapel for our private prayers and she herself prayed there every day during the rest hours. Miss Tell also taught divinity throughout the school, beginning each lesson with a prayer. She dictated notes, a removed and awesome person, and my first notebooks, written with a trembling hand, bear witness to my fear of her. But what she taught was familiar to my sister and myself and passages from the Bible, heard over and over again in church at Harewood, we now found we knew by heart.

Even Miss Tell was impressed. One evening at our bed-time she summoned us to her study. We stood in dressing gowns and slippers while she questioned us about the religious teaching we had received at home. 'You have been well taught' was her judgment, and she dismissed us, giving us little books of prayers for our private use.

Every morning all the school met for prayers in the Hall; we sang a psalm as well as hymns and listened to a Scripture reading. Once a week the local clergyman who was our chaplain gave us a talk as well. Every evening there were prayers for the boarders in the Chapel. On Sunday mornings there was Sunday school as well as our weekly visit to the church in the town and, again in the Chapel, evensong.

'Now lettest thou thy servant depart in peace.'

Somewhere, too, Miss Tell fitted in confirmation classes. But the younger children saw another side of her nature when on Sunday evenings they crowded into her study where, delightfully and delightedly, she read to them from *Pollyanna* and other happy children's books.

On the surface we bore with this surfeit of religion with amazing compliance. Unfailingly the lines of silent girls filed into Hall or Chapel morning and evening. To miss evening Chapel was risky, but possible; but to escape morning prayers was out of the question. Every girl had to answer to her name with the formula, 'Adsum. Good morning', as she passed through the portico on her way to the Hall. Those who, such as the Roman Catholics, were exempt from prayers, met under supervision.

We learnt to escape into our own thoughts, but there were some things we enjoyed. I loved the singing. And now lines of a hymn or psalm come back to me to fit my varying moods because they are carried with me from those days on the music of their chants and harmonies.

> 'I will lift up mine eyes unto the hills
> From whence cometh my help.'

> 'Because Thou hast been my Helper,
> Therefore under the shadow of Thy wings will I rejoice.'

I remember too with delight the read devotions at evening Chapel – the crystallized beauty of the ancient prayers and their inspiration. One prayer ran:

> 'Teach us, good Lord, to serve Thee as Thou deservest,
> To give and not to count the cost,
> To fight and not to heed the wounds …',

and there was another which surprised me because we asked for 'the spirit of gaiety' as well as for 'a quiet mind'.

In our first year a religious play was performed, directed by Miss Tell, depicting the story of the English saint, abbess of a monastery in Saxon times, where the rough herdsman Caedmon was moved to pious utterance in song. The setting of the play was inspired by Fra Angelico's painting of the annunciation, a print of which hung in our Chapel. The colours of the folded curtains that draped the stage matched the blue and ivory of the painting, and the scene was sparely furnished to resemble its uncluttered simplicity. The play summed up for me the spirit of the religion of the school, that of the piety of the cloister and the exaltation of the cathedral.

We kept Lent and learnt to give up something for the forty days – dancing in the Hall on Saturday nights, sweets, marmalade, even salt – rejoicing when we learnt that Sundays were not to be included in the days of fasting. But, however poorly we kept the spirit of the fast, I did gain something lasting from the regular exercise of abstinence, a kind of support in time of deprivation and a confidence that I can accept and bear it.

During Lent, too, we sang the story of the cross. Every Friday night of that season, at the evening Chapel service, the stark and vivid words, the poignant melody made inroads on our reluctant imaginations.

> 'See Him in raiment rent, with His blood dyed.
> Women walk sorrowing by His side.
> Is there no loveliness, you who pass by,
> In that lone figure which marks the sky?'

I strained feeling and imagination to bring them in tune with the atmosphere of this event. The cross. If one man's suffering, taken from among many, was so commemorated, there must be something extraordinary and different about it. I knew the explanation; I must have heard it many times, but the significance escaped me, for there was no soil of sacrifice or accepted suffering in which it could take root in my heart.

Did this religion come down to earth? Those who professed lived commendably, but they were reticent about God in everyday life, as if God, like nakedness, were in bad taste. But I part expected, when I brought my problems in confidence to someone who lived religiously, that I would hear about Him. I did find a considerate hearing and wisdom, but no-one said 'Pray', or 'He helped me in this way', and I was a little surprised, but also relieved.

Yet, although God did not seem immediate and instant in ordinary life, we did admit Him to be personal. For we sang:

> 'Jesu, my Lord, I Thee adore;
> Oh, make me love Thee more and more.'

But the personal seemed to be kept for special moments and states of mind: the end of the Communion service, the bowed knee, the fervent adoration. Was there no-one to show me that I could find Him in class when I was tense and fretful, that I could admit to Him the pride and pleasure of success and that He could teach me how to live with other people? Would I have been willing or ready to listen if one tried? Here and there a voice spoke of God in everything. One was George Herbert's. Often in morning prayers we sang his hymn, which began:

> 'Teach me, my God and King,
> In all things Thee to see,
> And what I do in anything
> To do it as for Thee!'

This was the message that was missing from my experience of religion; but here it came faintly, though it was persistent and was not to be dismissed. But I found I could evade it because the language was quaint and the application inappropriate. For the hymn continued:

> 'All may of Thee partake;
> Nothing can be so mean,
> Which, with this tincture, "for Thy sake,"
> Will not grow bright and clean.
>
> A servant with this clause
> Makes drudgery divine:
> Who sweeps a room, as for Thy laws,
> Makes that and the action fine.'

But I was not a servant; my burden at that time was not the drudgery or the meanness of my duties, and I forgot the message because the illustration was irrelevant. Still I considered the message as we sang the hymn from time to time, and found it hard to believe that God cared about ordinary daily activities – drudgery least of all. About worship, 'good works', unselfishness, truthfulness, I was sure He did care. But about games, and geometry, and bed-making, how could He care? Perhaps, I thought, He cared about unhappiness. But I hid from Him the things that gave me pleasure for I feared that He would take them away. God seemed to enter almost only into the gloom and misery in human experience and to have nothing to say in approval of success and ambition and the joy of living, and Bunyan (reluctantly I admit it) stood for me then as the prophet of this message. I found *Pilgrim's Progress* bare and drab; the country through which Christian passed, in my mind's eye, was treeless and flowerless; no music or laughter lightened his journey, and I turned in deep revulsion from the grimness of Christian's experiences.

Other writers did strike a more positive note. On cheerful days we sang:

> 'God who created me
> Nimble and light of limb,
> In three elements free –
> To run, to ride, to swim!'

(I spent many puzzled moments on these two lines – unaided by explanation.)

> 'Not when the mind is dim,
> But now from the heart of joy
> I would remember Him!
> Take the thanks of a boy!'

I entered joyfully into the spirit of this song until the last line, when the awareness that we, who were offering the thanks of a boy, were one hundred women and girls of varying ages, disturbed the reality of our thanksgiving.

Another voice unobtrusively expressed what I longed for and needed in those days. In the dining room hung a prayer in verse, handwritten and decorated amateurishly in ink with drawings of flowers and spiralling lines. It had been left there from the days before my time at school, by someone who must have been warm and liberal in spirit. No-one ever drew our attention to this prayer; it hung apparently forgotten at the far end of the room by the back entrance near the kitchens. The strand of cold asceticism in the pattern of our life, and the strident voice of repressive discipline we were hearing around us, seemed to deny what it was saying. It began:

> 'Give me a good digestion, Lord,
> And also something to digest –
> But where and how that something comes
> I leave to Thee who knowest best.'

When I read this, otherwise censored images awoke in my mind of fresh, buttered bread at breakfast with delicious treacle-coloured marmalade made in the school kitchens, and home-made cakes on Sundays. So God was pleased to give what pleased my appetite. A little window of relief opened on the gloom and hardness in my heart and shut quickly again. I read on:

> 'Give me a point of view, good Lord,
> Let me know what is and why.
> Don't let me worry overmuch
> About the thing that's known as I.'

I hardly believed that God would allow me a point of view – this was more than Miss Hobbs would allow. The rest of that verse was beyond me; I knew too well that I must forget myself but my trouble was that I could not, and it seemed a contradiction, that I could have a point of view and yet not worry about myself. The prayer ended:

> 'Give me a sense of humour, Lord.
> Give me the power to see a joke,
> To get some happiness from life
> And pass it on to other folk.'

How I needed to have this petition granted!

CHAPTER XII

After I had been at school four terms, I experienced my first moral crisis. It came about in this way. Friday was the weekly day of reckoning. After school prayers the headmistress read the week's list of good and bad points. Girls who had been particularly rude or disobedient, or even worse, deceitful, were singled out and chastised publicly. It was awesome. Miss Tell held her audience enthralled, as by word and expression she showed the blackness of our wrongdoing and upheld the ideals the school stood for. In her emotion she might pace across the platform; the rest of the room would swim about my eyes while I held her figure in focus. To be disgraced in prayers was so unbearable an idea to me that I did not even consider it possible. I managed to keep out of trouble, though I was never quite sure but that one day the accusing eye would be fixed on me. As long as I was not involved, however, I could even find some entertainment in the Friday ordeal. In a week of uneventful routine, Friday morning gave some excitement to life. I went into prayers as one might go to a cinema to see some exciting, if rather frightening, film.

One day during the rest hour when we were meant to lie in silence on our beds there was general excitement for some reason so that girls continued speaking after the bell for silence. The disorder was marked enough to be reported to the headmistress and the dread order was given: anyone who broke silence must report to Miss Tell. To break silence was to communicate by sign as well as to speak, and on this fateful occasion I had made a sign.

I could not face public disgrace. To know that I had done wrong was bad enough; to have it exposed before the school was intolerable. I argued with my conscience and did not own up. When those who had reported were lined up in front of the school the following Friday morning I envied and admired them. I envied them their moral realism, because it was easier for one who accepted the fact that she broke the rules from time to time to own up to one more failure. I admired their courage, and I envied them too, because their punishment was over. My punishment continued, my punishment of myself, and it was unbearable. Soon after, I had the first of a number of severe depressions which came at intervals over the next thirteen years. I had the sensation of being withdrawn from everything around me. I managed to act normally, but I lived in a nightmare and the dominant reality in that nightmare was the fact that I had not owned up to breaking silence.

After about a week or more of this suffering I made the tremendous decision to own up to one of the staff. I did not choose Miss Tell: she seemed too distant. I chose Miss Hobbs. My heart beat fast and my mouth and throat were dry as I approached the ordeal; beyond it lay release from torment and I could hardly wait for that. I owned up walking with her round the quadrangle after supper one evening. I heard none of the words she spoke for I was deaf with relief and joy. I gathered two things from what she said and only these mattered: she understood completely the ordeal I had been through and, joy of joys, she was not going to make a public spectacle of me or punish me further in any way. I still feel grateful to her for what seemed to me at the time a magnificent act of mercy. But I gained little from this experience. I was not humbled. I set my teeth and resolved that this would never happen again: I would make sure I kept the rules. I did not come to see myself as prone as anyone else to do wrong things – I could not. I had to see myself as capable of being good and perfect – this was one of the props of my life, the other being my determination to excel at lessons.

I had to hold on to these props, for I had lost the others. Particularly did I miss my home; I missed my parents, the sanity of home life, my father's good sense and reasonableness, the warmth and closeness of my mother. By contrast, school was a barren place emotionally. I longed for my mother. I wanted to put my arms around her neck and feel her soft cool skin against my face. At St Hilary's all physical contact was forbidden: 'pawing and mauling' were not allowed; girls might not even hold hands, and to put an arm round another's waist was considered beyond the pale. Such behaviour was discouraged because it savoured of sentimentality, which was openly spoken against, or might lead to something worse, which was never mentioned.

In addition my parents had been, until now, a shield for us against the hardness of the 'outside' world. At Harewood they had been with us everywhere, both at home and at school. Now suddenly at the age of twelve we were completely cut off from them. We were not let down gradually. Nothing made up for this loss. Here at school I knew that people cared, but that was not enough.

Yet deeper than the strain of moral conflict and the poverty of emotional relationships was the spiritual uneasiness that I had begun to feel at Harewood, and which came to a climax at school. When I was thirteen we read Francis Thompson's poem, 'The Hound of Heaven', in a poetry lesson:

> 'I fled Him, down the nights and down the days;
> I fled Him, down the arches of the years;
> I fled Him, down the labyrinthine ways
> Of my own mind; and in the mist of tears
> I hid from Him, and under running laughter …
> From those strong Feet that followed, followed after.'

At once I saw myself and my inner struggle, in the printed page before me. I, too, was flying from Him. I, too, knew something of trying to seek satisfaction in God's good gifts and in His creatures rather than in Himself, and ominously the poem spoke of disappointment in these things:

> 'I pleaded, outlaw-wise,
> By many a hearted casement, curtained red,
> Trellised with inter-twining charities; …
> But, if one little casement parted wide,
> The gust of His approach would clash it to: …
> But still within the little children's eyes
> Seems something, something that replies,
> *They* at least are for me, surely for me!

> I turned me to them very wistfully;
> But just as their young eyes grew sudden fair
> With dawning answers there,
> Their angel plucked them from me by the hair.
> "Come then, ye other children, Nature's – share
> With me" (said I) "your delicate fellowship" ...
> So it was done: ...
> Heaven and I wept together, ...
> But not by that, by that, was eased my human smart.'

As we went through the poem I hated it; it made me come face to face with what I knew was the basic issue in my life, and that issue was undecided. I did not want to meet Him; I was afraid of Him. This gave a bottomlessness to my life that overthrew every pleasant experience, every ambition and prideful satisfaction and made it worthless. I could be happy only as long as I could forget this crucial issue.

The last stanza of the poem was a complete surprise:

> 'Now of that long pursuit
> Comes on at hand the bruit;
> That Voice is round me like a bursting sea:
> "And is thy earth so marred,
> Shattered in shard on shard?
> Lo, all things fly thee, for thou fliest Me!
> Strange, piteous, futile thing! ...
> All which I took from thee I did but take,
> Not for thy harms,
> But just that thou might'st seek it in My arms.
> All which thy child's mistake
> Fancies as lost, I have stored for thee at home:
> Rise, clasp My hand, and come!" '

As I read on to the end I caught my breath. For a tiny moment I could see the possible end of my struggle and desperate condition. It was too good to be true.

> 'Halts by me that footfall:
> Is my gloom, after all,
> Shade of His hand, outstretched caressingly?

"Ah, fondest, blindest, weakest,
I am He Whom thou seekest!
Thou dravest love from thee, who dravest Me." '

I had not arrived there, but the poet had come to that place. I hardly dared to hope that one day I, too, would turn and find that my pursuer was Love.

CHAPTER XIII

A new library was built soon after I came to St Hilary's. It was thoughtfully placed in a quiet corner with west-facing windows so that the sun streamed in only in the cool afternoon. It was restful in colour, the light brown tones of the woodwork contrasting only gently with the cream-coloured walls, and variety was added by the leafy patterning of the seat covers.

I wandered into the library one afternoon and aimlessly leafed through an encyclopaedia. There was a section on the negro. I turned to it with interest. Negro! Unmentioned subject! It had almost the same effect as sex. I read,

'The negro in certain … characteristics … would appear to stand on a lower evolutionary plane than the white man, and to be more closely related to the highest anthropoids.'[*]

The writer continued:

'Mentally the negro is inferior to the white … We must necessarily suppose that the development of the negro and white proceed on different lines. While with the latter the volume of the brain grows with the expansion of the brain pan, in the former the growth of the brain is on the contrary arrested by the premature closing of the cranial sutures and lateral pressure on the frontal bone. This explanation is reasonable … but evidence is lacking on the subject and the arrest or even deterioration in mental development is no doubt very largely due to the fact that after puberty sexual matters take the first place in the negro's life and thoughts … The mental constitution of the negro is very similar to that of a child, normally good-natured and cheerful, but subject to sudden fits of emotion and passion during which he is capable of performing acts of singular atrocity, impressionable, vain, but often exhibiting in the capacity of servant a dog-like fidelity which has stood the supreme test.'

[*] *The Encyclopaedia Britannica*, 11th edition, 1910–1911, XIX, 344–348.

There was more. I did not read it all. I put the book away and left the library. I was wordless and numb inside. The idea of discussing this with anyone else did not occur to me – or at least, this was out of the question for I assumed that everyone else was involved painfully in the question of race and colour as I was. One just did not talk about these things.

I knew in a dim way that what I had read about the inferior intelligence of the negro was not supported by the evidence, at least in Jamaica. Here at school the girls of negro origin were often more successful than white girls as the former in many cases entered on scholarships and the latter because their parents could afford the fees, whatever their ability. But whatever the evidence in the small world around me, here was a statement to the opposite effect in the authoritative pages of the school encyclopaedia. There must be in the larger world and among people of learning, for whom I had great respect, many people who shared this belief about the intellectual inferiority of the negro race and I could not help feeling there must be some truth in it, some basis or fact on which they held this belief. I felt condemned. There were people in the world who would assume I was, by virtue of my race, inferior in intellect. It became terribly important to me to demonstrate to myself and to other people that this was not true.

CHAPTER XIV

I left school in December 1949 when I was eighteen. My goal was to go to university, to university in England. The University College of the West Indies had started the year before in Jamaica, but I had always looked forward to going to England and I would consider nowhere else.

My sister had won a five-year scholarship on her results in the Higher Schools Certificate examination. She was going to read French in London University. I could not afford to go but eventually I felt I must find a way. In the meantime what could I do? I was full of hope but I had no immediate plans. My sister did not take up her scholarship straight away but she was asked to teach temporarily in a teacher training college. When the first term of 1950 began I was on my own at Harewood.

My parents began teaching again, my sister was away at her new post, my friends were back at school. The world of St Hilary's, in which I had been carried along by the steady pace of activities and in which I had a well-defined place in the strata of authority, was closed to me and I was lost without it. The term went by. The holidays began and my sister returned home, but she was not the same. Until now we had always been together; we had a shared knowledge of most things in our lives, places, people, experiences; we understood each other almost completely. But now she knew people and had experiences which I did not share. Another important part of my world was shrinking away from me.

In the second term, however, she invited me to spend a week with her at the college; I was to stay in a private house nearby. I looked forward to this – to knowing the world she now lived in which I did not share. But I found that going to visit her in this situation was quite different from sharing in the situation with her on the same footing. I was there beside her in the flesh but I had no part in the life she was now living. I met as a casual acquaintance people with whom she was involved in a continuing relationship. The consciousness of shared experience which had lasted almost unbroken since our infancy was cut off. Again I was plunged in severe depression, and again this took the form of a spiritual crisis.

The outcome of the first crisis at school when I was driven to own up to breaking a rule and concealing it, was a determination that never again would I do anything dishonest which I might be driven by my conscience to confess to someone else. I was able to keep a fairly exact check on my sins because of the practice of self-examination which I began after my confirmation and for which I was equipped with a list of questions based on the Ten Commandments. I worked very hard at avoiding lying and dishonesty – sins which involved other people and required confession to them. The more vague sins such as pride I was not entirely complacent about, but at least they did not involve shameful exposure to other people. I found I kept admitting time after time to the same sins, and there were some I could do nothing about.

It happened that as I travelled by bus to see my sister at the training college I looked out at the almost uninhabited countryside we were passing through – up at the sky and the dark, blue-green hills jagged with overgrown bush and rock and trees – and my struggle came to a head in these words: 'How can I believe in a God who sent me into a world into which I did not ask to be born and will punish me in hell for sins which I cannot help committing?'

This did not mean that I was considering atheism or agnosticism. I was not questioning the existence of God. Rather, I was throwing out a challenge in bitterness and resentment to God to vindicate His nature – to prove that He was a loving and just God in spite of what appeared to me to be His injustice and hardness. I was once more shut up to myself in a formless, wordless misery. It lasted all the time I was visiting my sister. I went through the motions of meeting people and appearing pleased and interested in what I saw, but I was dead and heavy inside.

Even food was tasteless. The one thing that pierced my senses in that time was the taste of tomatoes. It was tomato-growing country and every day there were cooked tomatoes at one meal or another. The sight of the small, squashed, red-orange forms lying limp in their juice mingled with fat, and their sharp acid-sweet taste remained with me long afterwards, strengthening the memory of that time and standing for the horror of it.

The cloud lifted when I returned to Harewood. There was the hope of something to do. I was to teach a younger cousin privately as his home. The day before I began I had a telegram. It was from St Hilary's, from the acting headmistress: 'Can you come tomorrow – start Wednesday.' Today was Monday. Life opened out before me again. I was being asked to teach at my old school. Back to people and a situation I knew. But I was going back to the staff! I wasted few misgivings on this. Somebody thought I could do it. Perhaps I could. The next evening I was at the school being briefed for my first lesson next morning. The maths teacher had been taken ill and the need for a replacement was desperate.

For three years I 'filled in' at St Hilary's because the number of girls was increasing and the staff shortage was chronic. I was busy on familiar ground and this more than made up for the underlying conflicts in myself and the failures in my relationships with people round me.

The religious battle grew fiercer. I had a steady boyfriend. He encouraged my religiosity and I became more Anglo-Catholic in practice, saying set prayers at regular hours, keeping fast-days and feast-days, scourging my soul with lists of self-examination, going to church services twice on Sundays and at least once during the week, as well as the daily services in the school. Yet at the same time this friendship with its mutual interest in religion was at the centre of my conflict with God. I was trying to keep God out of my life: I offered Him my services in terms of regular prayer and churchgoing, self-denial and even a dutiful struggle against the sins I acknowledged; but I could not, I would not, let Him order my life.

Least of all would I listen to Him on the matter of this particular friendship. I knew God was urgently saying something to me about it but I would not listen. I assumed He was saying, 'Give it up'; I have since learnt that sometimes He is saying instead, 'Give it to Me.' I was caught in this relationship and I could not free myself, but I did not allow God to prove that He would free me. In a bitter corner of my heart simmered this thought: 'What does God care about human needs and feelings except to thwart and deny them?' This was my idea of God, demanding, hard to please, too far beyond me in His greatness and perfection to care about the details of my life.

What or who was I? Increasing self-examination showed me that I would never get to the end of my sin. I gave up blatant lying only to find more subtle forms of deceit in myself. I strained at these petty sins and swallowed the greater sins of attitude, ignoring the one great sin of saying 'No' to God and closing my ears to Him. But I feared to say 'Yes' to God. If I did and gave Him everything, what would I have but emptiness; what unknown sacrifices would I have to make?

Christine, another member of staff, had a room next to mine. She was baffling because she was different. Now I know why: God was inside her. She was human and faulty, plainly weak in some respects, like the rest of us; yet something moved her and kept bursting out from her in unexpected ways. When she came into a room, doubtful or malicious conversation stopped, and at the end of the day, she was ready to go out to the children to enjoy them and work with them, when I turned wearily in on myself and looked for someone else to sustain me.

Christine lent me a copy of the book *For Sinners Only*, the exposition of the teaching and practice of the Moral Rearmament group. When I read it I was once again engulfed in another severe attack of depression. I could not sleep at night, I could not lie in my bed. I knelt in the darkness on the bare polished floor of my top-storey room at St Hilary's with lofty rafters in the unceiled roof where a croaking lizard moved its fat, grey body soundlessly along. I knelt and I knew like a taste or a touch, like some physical reality – blackness and bottomlessness. Despair, death, the grave, hell, something of all these were there. The book, *For Sinners Only*, that brave account of men trying to pull themselves up and make themselves pure and good, perfect and right, was for me a huge mockery. I had tried to do this and I had failed.

On this occasion I did confide in one person: someone who I felt would understand suffering of this kind. She was Miss Hobbs, the one to whom I had owned up seven years before at my first experience of this agony. She agreed that God could not want me to suffer like this. But why did He allow it? Why could I not break through to His forgiveness and healing and love? There was no need to ask. I was only too ready to take His best gifts and turn away from Him, the giver. I would not give Him myself. He could not give me His love. Year after year, week after week, I heard and read and sang of the Son of God who loved me and gave Himself for me, and I was as far from experiencing that love as if I had never heard of Him. In spite of all the knowledge of the Gospel story in my head I still asked, 'What does the cross mean?'

At about this time, the first summer school in Jamaican arts and drama was being held at Knox College in Christiana. There the earth is red and the cool, keen air gives brightness and sharpness to colour, to the greenness of the grass and of the hillside, to the blue of the sky. We sang Jamaican songs, acted plays on Jamaican life, tried painting and sculpture, were inspired to social work. We were young Jamaicans seeing the beginning of forms of drama and art and writing which were our own, not handed on from other cultures but our own, blended out of the widely sprung streams of language and music that make up our past. It was a thrilling time. There was so much buoyancy, so much hope, surely there was also certainty about the deepest issues?

'What does the cross mean?' I asked a theological student there (why did I think his label gave him authority and wisdom?). He groped for a reply. His companion spoke up quickly, 'Haven't you read books …?' The conversation died. There was too much happening for me to mind deeply, but I had been let down. I felt uneasy; I was disappointed. I learnt the answer to my question two years later in the chill, grey drizzle of London in autumn and then I was ready to receive it.

Though I was divided in myself, seeking God in part and in part holding on to my own way, yet God gave me one freedom. Every week I chose one sin which I would try to rid myself of. I thought that by self-discipline over a set period I could put behind me one sin after another and in this way eventually reach some perfect state – at least as to the more clear-cut sins, such as dishonesty, lying, impurity. I did not attempt to remake my attitudes. In this futile struggle (for the old sins, after a short subjection, emerged again like weeds) I suddenly realized one day that I was not bound to give in to sin – that though the impulse came I no longer went on inevitably to put it into action. I could stop and choose between the right and the wrong, between the angry outburst and the quiet answer, that I could hold back from that last morsel which meant greed – if I chose. Before, I had no choice; the sinful impulse was put into action in one unbroken and inevitable movement but now I had a new power at least over the sins I admitted and tried to fight against. It was a power that took me by surprise. I accepted it happily. To whom I owed it and by what means I had arrived at it, I did not stop to question.

Until now St Hilary's, its way of life, its values and standards gave me the pattern of life which I accepted. More than this, I accepted this pattern as the way in which life ought to be lived. I did not feel safe outside this world. But even while I was teaching there, I began to see beyond and outside this world and to free myself from the hold it had on me. I became aware of this because of one evening's experience.

Market Town, above which St Hilary's stands, is set in the hills of St Ann and lies near the north coast of Jamaica. About two miles out of the town the land falls away sharply and the road descends to the narrow plain below, to the white sands and the sea. In the early 1950s long stretches of the beach were still open to the public. The building of seaside hotels which has claimed the north shore beaches almost exclusively for the tourist, had just begun. The wide new highway, now sweeping closer inland to give room for tourist development near the sea, was not yet even talked of; its humbler predecessor still curved along the seaside, as often as not quiet and deserted.

On a moonlit night a few of us members of St Hilary's staff left the school, left the pressures of being responsible for other people's daughters, the tensions of the staff room and the toil of

marking exercises, and went by car along this road to the beach –
empty except for a palm tree and a few scuttling crabs. We parked
the car by the roadside, stepped over the low wall and on to the
sands where we frolicked like children. The sands, the sea and the
sky were incredibly full of light; behind us were the dark shadows
cast by the wall and the palm tree. No-one could question our
right to be there. As far as we could see there was no light from a
house, there were no other people. On either hand stretched the
sand, before us was the open sea. Lifting my head, I breathed in
the warm and tingling air. Instead of the echo of footsteps and
voices which we heard from day to day within the walls of the
school, we now heard only the movement of the sea in the wide
spaces.

The spell broke. In a few moments we had lived long and richly.
Subdued we turned back to the car, back to our duty, to put on our
dignity as teachers again. Tomorrow the rigour of bells and the
timetable, the hierarchy of relationships, the ritual, the formulae
of behaviour, would close in on us and mock us in our bondage:
'This is the sum total of reality. Nothing exists except St Hilary's.'
But now we could laugh at that voice, for not far away we knew
that the sea and the air sweep freely, and along the sands by the
road there are no people.

The world of people – that was where the trouble lay. I could
see this now: that when I set aside the narrow world of St Hilary's,
its ritual and formulae, I faced a deeper trouble in myself and in
my relationships with other people.

CHAPTER XV

'Tennis?' said someone in the staff room to me. 'You don't get the chance to play? Why don't you come along and join the club?' She was jaunty and friendly, and she obviously was sincere in her invitation. But though she was English, surely she had lived in Jamaica and in Market Town long enough to *know* ... Did she not know, had she not realized? But she was so wrapped up in her music perhaps it had escaped her. How refreshing – and embarrassing – to meet someone who had not realized that the tennis club in Market Town admitted only whites and near-whites! Of course I would not dream of going to the tennis club! Someone else suggested that I go and seek membership there as a test of this unwritten colour bar. I had been once to the club, once to a dance at night under subdued lights which are flattering to the complexion and where pleasure blurs the vision of the onlooker. But to go in the hard light of afternoon and face the scrutiny of my person and the challenge as to my antecedents was unpalatable. In any other situation I would have gone to battle, but here I was weak and unwilling as if I agreed with this rejection of my person, because my skin was too brown, my hair so kinky that it had to be straightened.

Colour. Class. I seemed to meet them everywhere. I wished I could escape them. I could not change my colour. I did not want to, not really. I wanted to remain myself and be accepted. I longed to find some company in which I could enjoy the good things I sought after, the tastes and interests I aspired to, and still remain myself. But while I looked outside myself for status and acceptance, the trouble lay within myself.

That year I found a poem in Madeline Kerr's new book, *Personality and Conflict in Jamaica*. It was by Vera Bell, a Jamaican; she was writing about her ancestor the African slave, *my* ancestor:

'Ancestor on the auction block
Across the years your eyes seek mine
Compelling me to look
I see your shackled feet
Your primitive black face
I see your humiliation
And turn away
Ashamed

Across the years your eyes seek mine
Compelling me to look
Is this mean creature that I see
Myself
Ashamed to look
Because of myself ashamed
Shackled by my own ignorance
I stand
A slave

Humiliated
I cry to the eternal abyss
For understanding
Ancestor on the auction block
Across the years your eyes meet mine
Electric
I am transformed
My freedom is within myself.'

Matthew Arnold wrote this of Goethe's poetry:

'He put his finger on the spot
And said, "Thou ailest here and here".'

Vera Bell's poem did this for me. I saw myself; she showed me my
ailment and the remedy. Before, I could not bear to look into my
background. Now I dared to look. Just to say to myself, 'My great-
great-grandparents were black slaves' this alone was releasing. In
my imagination I looked in turn at the people whose colour and
social position I coveted and I dared to admit to my black ancestry. This was only in my imagination but it was painful enough, and
releasing. My ancestor stood for everything that I rejected in

myself, my racial self, my social, cultural self. His was the black face that I saw everywhere and passed over. While I denied him, he destroyed my peace and I was unstable. Now I accepted him and I was more at peace. But I held him as inferior still and not as equal. I no longer turned myself from him but it was painful to invite him in and acknowledge him as part of myself. My freedom was still only partly won; my peace was uneasy.

So far I had gained two freedoms – a certain power to choose the good when tempted to do wrong, and in a measure the freedom that comes from self-acceptance. These gave me confidence that I could wrest and struggle and achieve whatever I set myself to do. I allowed no misgivings about my ability to do this. I hoped and looked for nothing beyond myself.

CHAPTER XVI

My sister went to London University two years before I did. Her letters home were full of vivid detail and enthusiasm. She had met, she said, a group of Christians whose faith was living and real. She seemed to be becoming more religious. My heart sank. To me this meant saying more prayers, attending more church services, adding more duties and self-denials to a life already straitened and made grim by a multiplicity of 'Thou shalts' and 'Thou shalt nots'. I dreaded going to join her. Her letters became more dominated by the religious theme and usually contained a paraphrase of the most recent Sunday morning sermon by Dr Martyn Lloyd-Jones of Westminster Chapel. My mother enjoyed these letters. I turned away from them, put off reading them and then skimmed quickly over the sermon.

The day came when I set off to join her. All my savings went into the cost of the boat passage to England. My parents undertook to pay my college fees and boarding expenses and my sister offered to share her scholarship allowance with me for other necessities. It was another venture of faith, but I was neither anxious nor awed by what lay ahead. I had the ignorance and the buoyancy of the adolescent and the sacrifices of my family I accepted as my due. I was going up to university and this was all that mattered. My hope was to be realized. I did not expect it to be otherwise.

There were only about twenty passengers in the banana boat. We were all second-class passengers. 'The bananas', said the crew, 'are the first-class passengers.' A number of us were going to England as students, among them Marcus Garvey, son of the outstanding Jamaican of the same name, who was going to London to read law. We sat at the Captain's table, Garvey sitting at the place of honour on his right. The Captain, in his conversation, whether in earnest or not, often criticized Jamaica, and Garvey with seriousness and near anger at times suitably defended his country.

At the other end of the table, where I was sitting, the conversation was more light-hearted. The Chief Engineer, plump and persistently cheerful, teased us through the first gloomy seasick days; he was the centre of laughter and a source of funny stories. 'Never marry a sailor', he cautioned me (I was the only woman at the table). 'When a sailor says goodbye to his wife he pulls a long face, but as soon as he is round the corner and out of sight he starts whistling merrily – he is so happy to be going back to his ship. Never marry a sailor.' 'Not again,' I replied. Raised eyebrows and merry laughter greeted my reply. After a puzzled moment. I realized that I seemed to say 'Not again' as if I had once been married to a sailor. 'I mean, "Not after hearing this",' I explained, for this is how we use the phrase in Jamaica. So, in that moment, I saw clearly that, even after the process of Anglicization at St Hilary's, I still used idioms that were strange to English ears and I would need to continue the process of sifting and censoring my speech and of learning new forms, which had begun at school.

More grave and more reserved was the ship's doctor, though he shared in the comradely atmosphere. He was a spare, scholarly-looking man in his early forties. He was not a regular member of the crew but was on a 'busman's holiday' from his London practice; he doled out pills for seasickness and had a short morning surgery and sunbathed for most of the day. He wrote plays, he told me, and was preparing one to be broadcast by the BBC. He had the script on board; would I like to come up after dinner and look at it? If I had qualms about accepting his invitation, I silenced them before they surfaced. I wanted to forget the old restraints and proprieties – purely superficial they were! Here was a new life opening out before me. I was meeting a real, live playwright for the first time and I was to see his manuscript. How thrilling!

At about nine o'clock that evening I entered the doctor's cabin and he shut the door. I was surprised at how small and cramped it was. I had half expected a suite of rooms; instead there was his bunk opposite the door and on this side a cluttered work table with barely two feet of space between.

Did I drink? he asked. 'No.' Did I smoke? 'No.' No vices? 'Not yet', I replied; I was trying to appear sophisticated. There was little further conversation. I hardly remember looking at his manuscript. For, without much ado he began to make love to me. It was pleasant at first. Only gradually did I realize my predicament. What could I do? To shout or cry out was out of the question. Just beyond the porthole on the deck were my companions, the other students of my own age with whom I would be spending the rest of the voyage in constant contact. They must certainly not know about this. I dared not make a dash for the door or resist him for fear of arousing him further – to violence perhaps. Then I remembered a novel I had read from the sixth-form library in which the hero, finding himself alone with his beloved, was completely put off by her coldness. 'I could not take you, Mary,' he said. I proceeded like her to play dead. Quietly but very earnestly I remonstrated. To my astonishment this had no effect. He was completely absorbed in what he was doing and quite indifferent to me.

In that moment I learnt something about the relationship between men and women that I had not allowed for before: that to make love and to love could be quite separate. I had to acknowledge even in my desperation that he was a skilful love-maker but he had not the slightest regard for me or my wishes. I have never unlearnt that lesson. If the resentment and bitterness passed in time, the sadness still remains. The advantage has been a deeper gratitude than I might otherwise have felt, when eventually I found both together in marriage. These were the deepest marks left by that evening's adventure. Physically, I escaped and by the merest accident – because it was an unsuitable time of the month. He had his limits. I think he was also relieved to have a face-saving excuse for calling off the episode as my indifference taxed his ardour.

'You will come again in a few days', he said as he opened the door. ('I must play the game. I have not yet escaped,' I thought.) 'Perhaps', I said aloud, and managed to smile as I stepped out in to the cool air.

'What were you doing in the doctor's cabin? Teaching him psychology?' one of the students remarked as I joined them on deck. I tried to reply but he could hardly have heard what I said; he did not seem to mind that what I murmured was hardly a reply to his question. He asked nothing more. The ease and friendliness of their company comforted me. The cool air was refreshing. The darkness, the sea and the vast sky received my trouble and gave me calmness.

Thanks to my mother, I was aware in every detail of the disaster to my future plans which I had just risked and escaped. And how had I escaped? Through no virtue or cleverness on my part – but by an accident of time outside my control. Divided as I was in my heart in my attitude to God, there seemed only one conclusion: that I owed my escape to Him. The repeated formula of many a Sunday worship came to life in my mind and with true thanksgiving I sang the Te Deum.

I learnt more that evening. I lost a little faith in myself, in myself as a virtuous person. Had I not accepted his invitation and enjoyed his attentions at first? Another thought came to me with crippling coldness. How did the doctor see me? – no doubt as an easy-going coloured girl, no more. At best he might romanticize the image, Gauguin-wise, and see in me a dusky islander, warm and giving, against the background of palm trees and a tropical moon. This was not the image I wanted to give of myself. I groaned within, my pride punctured. I saw then that away from my country and among strangers I would be stripped of the status and imputed reputation that the labels of family name and St Hilary's gave me there. Later I came to see that this was good. These were some of the things which bolstered my self-esteem and came between me and God. Stripped of them, I was made ready to receive Him.

CHAPTER XVII

We landed in London in September 1953, in dull, damp London, impressively impassive, absorbing everyone into its life, marking everything with greyness and grime. The West Indian faces that met me were strange, puffed up and mottled-pink, not lean and tanned as they were at home. They took me on tubes and buses, hurrying, giving quick instructions. Why did they have to hurry so? Being a stranger is as bewildering and crippling as sudden illness.

I thought I would never learn to distinguish one street of grey towering buildings from another, and since these buildings and the grey blanket of cloud overhead hid the path of the sun, I lost the sense of east and west by which I knew where I was facing and where I was going. I missed the sight of distant horizons, I longed for the mountains of my own Jamaica and the warm clear nights when the sky is brilliantly packed with stars, or when the moonlight lies a rich yellow because no artificial light rivals it. Moreover, I found with cruel disappointment that the sun could shine and give no warmth.

At first all English faces looked alike, for my eye was used to the contrasting faces of my country, black, white, brown and yellow in colour, varied in feature and hair form because of the variety of types they represent: African, Portuguese, Jewish, French, Spaniard, Syrian, Chinese, Indian and British – mixed and un-mixed. Here in England all people seemed uniformly prosperous after the sight of beggars in our streets, with a hand stretched out to those of well-dressed ease, and the tin shacks of the very poor not far from spacious and luxurious houses.

I came to love London during my days as a student. I came to love the continuous sound of life that only grew less noisy in the early morning hours and the nights that were never ominous or thick with darkness as they could be at Harewood where the owl's cry was frightening, drums beat in the distance for a pocomania meeting, and the barking of dogs and the cries of night insects dominated the world of men.

Sunday after Sunday I rode through Whitehall and Trafalgar Square by bus and was thrilled at the actual sight of places I had seen before only in books and films, places linked with stories and events of interest and prestige. I felt secure in a world that had gone on for so long and for the time being this was not spoiled by the knowledge that life in London can be drab and lonely. But the happy memories have outlasted this knowledge: I remember a mild day of sunshine in Gray's Inn court when I came upon a model being photographed, a fair-haired, laughing girl, wearing blue and holding a mass of yellow daffodils – a splash of life and colour standing out against the contained grey dignity of the buildings round her.

I also remember my first visit to the City where I spent a morning, incredulous and absorbed, as I watched the bank messengers in brass-buttoned red coats and shortened top hats walk briskly in and out of doors, up and down steps, and through the narrow streets; they were shut in a garrisoned world of stone built high round them, and it seemed to me that time had not passed here since Dickens wrote, and some barrier of immunity lay between this world and the changing, aching world massed outside it.

I shared a room with my sister in a university hall of residence in central London. The hall was graciously furnished and warm and we lived graciously. The order and formality reminded me of St Hilary's and I felt secure and at home. My mother paid my fees; my sister's scholarship allowance was generous and this she shared with me for buying clothes and lunches. But I could not afford to buy the books I needed for my course; I relied on the libraries and the student lending scheme of Messrs H. K. Lewis.

To increase my pocket money I sought a job and another student found one for me. Every Saturday morning I went by Underground to West Ham and with some trepidation took my place behind the counter of a market stall where cloth was sold. I passed the bales of cloth forward to the lanky, dark-haired salesman, who stood among his wares on the counter and harangued the passers-by, in confident and bracing Cockney, on the price and virtue of his goods. At lunch time I sat down with relief in a far corner by the laden shelves and ate my lunch of crisp flaky rolls that were too large, filled with slices of strongly flavoured sausage-meat. At the end of the day, with fifteen shillings payment, I made my way along the rubbish-littered streets and on to the tube, glancing round fearfully for 'Teddy' boys, until I emerged in relief at Russell Square and back to the haven of College Hall. Mercifully, before the days grew colder and darker, the Principal of the hall heard of my Saturday-morning outings and stopped them, offering me instead a bursary that made up for the loss of my small earnings, and freeing me to spend the time in study and needed relaxation.

Tentatively I began to explore what London and the university offered by way of recreation. I tried a concert for which two complimentary tickets were offered to the students in our hall of residence. It was very dull: 'Bach's five-finger exercises!' was my companion's comment, and the flicker of my enthusiasm died. It was barely smouldering enthusiasm. At St Hilary's I had ploughed miserably through five grades of pianoforte examinations, for I never mastered the knack of sight-reading; each piece I learnt laboriously, and strenuously memorized.

I enjoyed the musical performance of others, however. So did the rest of the school. The few crumbs of musical riches that fell to us we snatched at eagerly and with appreciation, whether it was the Jamaican baritone who sang to us or a concert by twelve-year-old Philippa Schuyler on a flying visit to the West Indies. At school I sensed a certain pressure on us to show enthusiasm for classical music though we had little opportunity to develop this, and I was determined not to pretend to an enjoyment I had not acquired for myself. Here in England I welcomed the chance to fill in the gaps in my musical experience, but I was put off by the chilling encounter with Bach at the beginning of my college days and I gave up the attempt until the opportunity came again in marriage with the contagion of my husband's enjoyment of good music, the depth of bitter-sweet experience and the regular ministrations of the BBC's Third Programme.

For physical exercise I chose the college hockey and country dancing clubs. In both my stay was short. It was cold standing on the field waiting to be placed in the hockey team. Besides, I had joined these activities to make friends but the thin, irregular ration of friendliness that came my way was unsustaining. Had I wanted exercise only I could have touched my toes twice daily in my study bedroom, but I wanted also the sense of belonging to a group where enjoyment of activity is increased by being shared. Perhaps I would have persisted through the bleakness of the early days if my zeal for either of my chosen activities had been great, but neither my natural ability nor my early associations had made it so.

At St Hilary's my introduction to hockey had been punctuated by the barbed and blasé comments of the expatriate games mistress who taught it: 'You Nation child, don't use your seat as a battering ram!' I was not her sole target. 'You over there with two pigtails and no manners!' was another of the memorable thrusts of this fair, rounded export of the English second drawer (her brother, she informed us, had been private secretary to Sir Winston Churchill). But her words could convey not only her own bad temper but the kindlier intent of stirring up our drooping spirits. When we faced her for country dancing on a Friday evening with drawn, weary faces, she would begin, 'Come on, cheer up! The Chinese have a proverb: "Even this day will pass"!' and by the end of the lesson we would be prancing gaily to the tune of the 'Dashing White Sergeant'. My memories of country dancing at St Hilary's are of the delight and abandoned relief it afforded at the end of a week of gruelling study.

But here at college, in a dismal, prefabricated hut, country dancing was stern business. The participants were nearly as neglectful of friendliness as the hockey players and were even more dedicated. Among them was a russet-haired couple, complete in kilt and tartans. For them, I guessed, the honour of Scotland depended on their strict performance of the ritual of the Scottish reel. I stayed a little longer with the country dancers than with the hockey players, and then gradually drifted away.

I was forced to conclude that my English fellow-students and I differed perhaps in the things that gave us pleasure, and certainly in the spirit in which we took our recreation. The Psychology Department gave a party before Christmas. There was music, and dancing was clearly intended, though the staff and older students stood round the sides of the room drinking beer. Bravely, two or three couples took to the centre of the room and performed self-consciously, without joy or ability, the current antecedent of the 'twist'. It was an embarrassing spectacle. Why did they dance if they could not, did not want to, or did not enjoy it? I was relieved when they gave this up, but also disappointed. I longed to dance as we would at home – because we enjoyed moving to music, arriving at one's preferred style of dancing and finding a partner to suit, not bound to waltz to a waltz or writhe to the rumba, so long as one moved in rhythm with the beat of the music and above all delighting in it.

We escaped from the dingy basement room of the 'party' out into the dimness of the quiet London square. In the deserted street, a police 'No Waiting' sign stood out temptingly. The others seized it and dragged it back to the department, while I looked on nervously. They did not keep their trophy long. The next day the Professor, who was American, demanded its restoration, conjuring up a picture of his reputable department being invaded by the CID, sternly intent on apprehending the miscreants. They returned it, a little abashed at being taken so seriously, retaliating with mild derision at his un-English anxiety over a minor student escapade, which they were sure the London policeman would handle with light-handed tolerance and view with patronizing good humour.

My English fellow-students seemed more at home in 'ragging' than at parties. At a safe distance I entered into their enjoyment of the turmoil when University College students captured 'Reggie', the mascot of King's College, the 'other place' to which we were traditionally opposed. And I can still be convulsed by the memory of the day when students brought all traffic to a standstill round the Aldwych. In this loop of roadway that surrounds Bush House, and into which the traffic flows from Kingsway, the Strand and Waterloo Bridge, there are usually policemen to control the flow and metal hurdles stacked there to bar the entrances when necessary. The students, having discovered a time of day when no policemen were about, arrived there concealed in grotesque animal costumes. Using the hurdles to block all entrances to traffic, they galloped round that meeting place of busy London streets while the public waited helplessly.

Living with my sister I watched her closely. What did her new religious zeal mean? The day after I arrived was a saint's day by the Church of England Calendar. Would she rise early and go to church? She did not. I was amazed and relieved to realize that the change in her was not increased religiosity; it was a change in the quality of her religion. I was interested.

Early that term there was an Inter-Varsity mission to the university. I went willingly with her to the meetings. The Missioner was an Anglican clergyman, a graduate, and he spoke of personal religion and conversion. I was astonished at the combination! Here was intellect that did not defy or cast doubt on God and here was traditional religion that was alive, personal and zealous to win others. What I heard and saw stripped me further of my defences. I was like a diver poised at the water's edge. All my life seemed to lead up to this moment. I could go back but I went on.

I asked to see the Missioner. 'I want to be a Christian', I told him. 'I have been sitting on the fence too long, but ...' But I was still afraid, afraid of being made to look a fool, afraid of being made to do what went against the grain. Not long before someone on a bus had asked me, 'Are you saved?' It was obviously a painful duty for him and I resented the question coming so bluntly from a stranger. Was this what being a Christian would mean, accosting and offending other people? On the boat I had seen Christians reading Bibles on the open deck; I preferred to keep my times of prayer private. 'Coward', said a voice, 'you'll never make a Christian.'

I put my problem in these words: 'I want to be a Christian but I do not want to do anything that is in bad taste.' I was answered before the Missioner replied, for good taste expressed itself in every detail of his dress and manner. 'Do you think', he replied, 'that God would ask you to do anything that was in bad taste?' I was well answered. The idea was incongruous. So it was possible, I realized, to be myself, to keep my tastes and preferences and be a Christian. God was not asking me to do violence to myself; He was not going to force me into an alien mould. Another hurdle was removed.

The Missioner continued, 'Go to your room, kneel down and ask Jesus to come into your heart and believe that He has come.' I did. I asked Him to come in and I believed He did. Every day I prayed on the assumption that He had. I set myself resolutely to accept that as a fact. I had come off the fence for good. I was determined to remain a Christian. It was an act of will. There was no feeling, no emotion. This part of me was still untouched. The longing, yearning self that sought love and friendship and could be moved by beauty was still mine and kept apart from God. He was still confined to the duty hut, the place of morals.

God was not going to force me into another mould but He began to change me from the inside. The times of prayer and Bible reading which had been a grim duty began to be times of quiet pleasure and satisfaction. Something was different about my attitude to religion. I learnt little that was altogether new, for I had learnt a great deal about the Bible and Christian doctrine at Harewood and St Hilary's. But I came to see these truths differently and what I had strained at before became clear and simple because I knew it in my own experience.

I sampled the religious societies, starting with the Student Christian Movement. Of this I remember little except earnest *tête-à-têtes* on current social issues with a fresh-faced, fair-haired youth (who was the President or the Secretary), on occasions when we were the only two who turned up to a meeting. I joined the Christian Union instead. My sister was already entrenched here and the arrival of her twin was (I have no doubt) avidly awaited. Here was friendliness, a welcome, well-supported meetings and a clear purpose. I went regularly but I was hardly a model member.

Sometimes the meetings clashed with a lunch-hour lecture which afforded the only opportunity to hear a brilliant lecturer and I skipped the meeting, perhaps to hear Professor J. Z. Young unfold with deceptive simplicity his experiments with octopuses to demonstrate that they can remember. At the lunch-hour meetings of the Christian Union, packets of sandwiches and cakes were sold for those who came straight from a lecture. These I found drab and dry. Instead, in the breathless minutes between lecture and meeting, I wove my guilty way through the smoke-filled basement den, which served as the student lounge in those days, past the noisy and the burly, the lank and the unshaven hoisting jugs of beer, and ordered a warm, moist hot dog at the bar which I topped with an apple.

On the other days at lunch in the college refectory, some members of the Christian Union sat together in a group by themselves. I avoided their company. Having spent three years teaching between school and university, I was older than any of them. I did not enjoy their jokes. Moreover, after St Hilary's I was wary of the beckoning of comfortable uniformity that subtly turns to tentacles of restrictiveness and railroads of prescription.

I discovered another West Indian whose company I preferred over lunch. Like myself he was older than most English students and he shared my passion for the Caribbean dialects, embellishing his conversation with wide gestures of his long-fingered hands. My companions in psychology were also older, having been required to spend a year at work before starting the course. I sat with them instead, or joined them on the prowl for new pastures that would vary the indifferent fare of the college refectory. We tried each student refectory in turn on Malet Street and thereabouts – Birkbeck College, the School of Tropical Hygiene – careless of the fact that we belonged to none of these, rejoicing in the blanket covering of the appellation 'student' and the liberating anonymity.

The most retiring of us, John Penrose, lost this anonymity soonest by becoming British chess champion for a number of years in succession. Only one other person had achieved this.

CHAPTER XVIII

There were new emphases in the sermons and talks I listened to. The particular emphasis of the group of Christians which I now joined was that of a personal relationship with God. Like Jacob, they 'wrestled' with God. They prayed simply and directly about the trivial and banal things of their lives, the immediate, personal things. I had kept these from God, partly because I did not want Him to interfere and partly because I did not really believe He cared about them. I still fought against this emphasis but I was attracted by it and began to accept it. I began to accept it because I was disillusioned about the emphasis I had embraced before – the emphasis on human moral and social responsibility, on 'big' causes, on organized good. Not that I now reject this emphasis; it challenges and inspires me still. But I found that it could stop short at words and plans, it could be wordy and ineffectual, and at that time, in my own life, this emphasis went side by side with personal failure. Then, I wanted realness and soundness *inside* myself, and, though it was costly, nothing else would do.

I also began to understand what the cross means; I came to appreciate the reality of evil, a powerful, personal evil pitted against God, and to see the cross as inevitable. God's love began to take shape as a reality, not a vague, sentimental influence. God's love meant that He was involved in a tremendous battle with a specific purpose – the wresting of men from the power of evil – and worked out in a specific way – the way of the cross. Why this repulsive, humiliating way?

I began then to understand and accept this, though it is still difficult. In the light of these glimmers of understanding my old quarrel against God faded. God was not at war with me, divine tyrant against human weakling; rather, He was involved in battle for my sake and the extent to which He seemed powerless and frustrated ('why doesn't God deliver me completely and instantly from all I cry to Him about?') was the measure of the power against which He was pitted and the measure of my own involvement in evil. ° When I saw this, resentment gave place to wonder and gratitude and the desire to give back to Him. And now I began to understand what the 'song and dance' of Easter is all about. I did not have to force myself to join in the song of triumph, the sense of triumph was beginning to burst out of my own heart. The bottomlessness of my periods of depression went out of my life. The ground under my feet was firm; I kept testing it. The firm ground that supported me was not myself; it was God, and His work in Christ.

I was shown and I saw the unity of the Bible converging upon and revolving round the person of Jesus Christ. This was the most exhilarating experience of my time at university: to see these truths afresh, to learn more and more about them and to share with other Christians the conscious knowledge of these truths and experiences.

Sunday became a different day, full of delight, leisurely, inspiring, and at the end of it I was ready to return to the week of work again. The day began unhurriedly with informal breakfast: hot coffee, rolls that broke in soft elastic ridges, crisp apples. Girls straggled into the dining room, hugging woolly sweaters, their faces pale without make-up, eyes unalert, unseeing.

We walked to church if it was fine – a long walk from Tottenham Court Road to Buckingham Palace Gate, which took us across deserted streets, past shop windows from which the gaudy, rigid models continued to stare through the heavy glass as they had stared through the busy Saturday and the almost silent night. We walked briskly, gay in each other's company, looking forward to the service so that we hardly noticed the distance that we walked or the grime of the small, high-walled streets. We hardly noticed our surroundings unless the crocuses were out in St James's Park, or a sloping green verge bounded by black railings outside an elegant Georgian house caught our attention, or the startling simplicity of the spire on All Souls' Church made the buildings round it, which bustled with life the day before, seem stale and earth-bound.

° Now I would say 'the measure of my own freedom to choose between good and evil'. *Then*, I was tremendously impressed by my own previous underestimation of the power of evil.

We made our way to Westminster Chapel where the large hall received us like a generous host, made ready, warm, carpeted, with seats of dark polished wood and with freshly painted walls in cream and gold and blue. The joy and eagerness with which we looked forward to these Sunday morning services were never disappointed. For me the complete break with an unvarying pattern of set psalms and prayers made me more alert to what I sang and heard. There was a set order and pattern in this service but the ingredients were changed every Sunday. We sang the quaint Scottish paraphrase of the Psalms that rhymed and made for easier singing, though they forfeited the style of the Prayer Book Version. The congregation abounded in young men, many of them students, so that the singing swelled heartily, though not only because it came from virile throats but also because, whether man or woman, old or young, we sang with heart as well as voice.

The sermon lasted up to forty minutes but this was a light burden to students used to hour-long lectures; our bodies were not worn down by drudgery and our minds were free from the distracting trivia of adult responsibilities. Besides, what we heard delighted us by the symmetry of its presentation and stimulated us by the depth of its content. We listened with fixed attention while the Doctor took a single phrase from Scripture and opened out a panoramic view of the spiritual world. He showed us the eternal issues that put our own world into perspective; God, working out His purposes that go beyond the scope of history, yet involved in history – a caring, knowing, loving God. We learnt of His anger and we were sobered but not resentful, and we could see where suffering has its place.

Yet it was not all sober truth and heavenly reality. Some members of the congregation stayed all day at the Chapel and in rooms behind the main Hall potatoes were baked and children played. Every Sunday we were reminded that we could stay and have cups of tea in the rooms adjoining the Chapel and the unvarying invitation to 'abide awhile in the precincts of the sanctuary' invariably amused us, given by the church secretary at the end of the notices, an elderly, silver-haired figure, dressed in tails and pin-striped trousers, with the round, sweet face of a Cheeryble brother.

CHAPTER XIX

The course I had chosen to follow at university was stimulating and enlightening. At home, the reaction to my choice of psychology had been, 'What will you do with it?' True, at that time there were no openings that I knew of for a psychologist in Jamaica, but I did not want to pursue further any of the subjects I had done at school and from my own reading I had developed an interest in this subject.

In my search for possible openings I had asked to see one of the psychiatrists at the mental hospital in Kingston, but he was discouraging. The period of training in psychiatry would be too long – seven or nine years. This was an unsuitable profession for a woman, and if I pursued it, marriage would be out of the question. I gave up the ambition to be a psychiatrist, but I was firm in my desire to go to university and my choice was eventually determined by the university which accepted me and the nature of the course it offered. I had to lay aside considerations of usefulness for the time being and choose entirely on the basis of my interests and in this I found complete support among my tutors and lecturers.

I gave all my attention and interest to the course and I enjoyed it immensely. There were disappointments, for I expected to be informed with certainty and I left with a host of unanswered questions. I had also half expected to gain deeper insight into the workings of my own mind and some guide to self-management, but this aim I quickly buried. The overriding aim of the department, aggressively pursued, was to place psychology among the sciences, and a science needed observables that could be objectively analysed and measured. Consideration of inner states of feeling and emotion, let alone moral and evaluative concepts, lay outside our field of inquiry. At first these seemed to be ruled out of existence altogether. The concept of 'mind' was questioned, found ephemeral, and dismissed. Instead we examined and described behaviour.

The herring gull that squawked in terror at the sight of a hovering enemy, sending its companions into flight, was described as reacting to a visual stimulus of specific proportions, with an emitted sound of so many decibels, which was in turn a signal for the flight reaction of its fellows. Human behaviour was described at the same level. We drew diagrams of young birds, animals and children demonstrating the disproportionate size of forehead over profile that evoked (it was alleged) the maternal response in the adult female of the lower species as well as in the human mother.

Was I only a higher animal, I asked myself, and was this all there was to me – reflex action and determined response? We were amused by Darwin's suggestion that the baying of dogs at the moon indicated an embryonic religious instinct, but he had set the pace: man was to be denied his unique character. Every experience, it seemed, was within reach of analysis and could be reproduced electrically or mechanically, however dearly we would cling to it and conceal it under the labels, 'aesthetic' or 'mystical'. The physiologist, by stimulating areas of the brain electrically, could evoke complex experiences of sight and sound – a colourful landscape or a musical composition, previously experienced or altogether new. The cyberneticians looked forward to the production of a super-complex machine that would simulate the whole range of human behaviour. Stimulus and response, electrical conduction, synaptical relay: the bared skeleton of my behavioural being rattled forlornly, until I reminded myself that these lecturers, who would so cold-heartedly divest me of my treasured humanity, themselves led lives subject to the forbidden categories. They fell in love, brought up their children to keep moral standards, exercised judgment, kept faith, showed compassion. Anyway, that supermachine was only a dream!

Part of the lot of a 'fresher' in the department of psychology was to be the 'subject' for the experiments of more advanced students. I was a fresher, hardly four weeks old, when a research student invited me to the attic of the building which housed our department where he made recordings of the electrical activity of the brain. He was investigating the large, slow, regular waves which occur during sleep, and as a sufficient number of suitable subjects in genuine slumber would have been difficult to come by, he was doing what he thought was the next best thing. He seated his subjects in a darkened room remote from the noise of traffic and people. Did he limit his definition of sleep to the absence of light and sound; or did he hopefully imagine that the alert fresher he might bring to this attic, to have electrodes pressed to his head from a large mysterious machine, would be likely to abandon himself to a state of mind in any way resembling the unguarded restfulness of sleep? As for me, with the memory of the ship's doctor still painfully near, the closed and darkened room, the male stranger, to say nothing of the electroencephalograph, threw me into a state of mental turmoil. To steady myself I furiously and soundlessly repeated nursery rhymes to myself. The readings of my cerebral activity must have resembled the recordings of a diversity of minor earthquakes! I am told his experiments came to nothing. Alas. Perhaps the wayward intangibles of inner states and individual past experience which he could not observe and control, and which naïvely he seemed to ignore, had something to do with this failure.

But the risk of failure of this sort the department was prepared to take. It was a small price to pay for the high prize of the admission of psychology to the status of a scientific study. They worked hard towards this goal. The professor rose at six in the morning and arrived early at the laboratories where he gradually lowered the body temperature of rats to study the effect of freezing on their ability to remember learnt activity. The lecturer from India who also worked with rats ran them through mazes regularly for weeks at a time without sparing himself, even on Sundays.

Accordingly they were at pains to cut the umbilical link with philosophy. In my first term I joined others from our department for a weekend at Cumberland Lodge, the Queen's 'grace and favour' house in Windsor Great Park, given for the use of university students. We shared the house that weekend with a party from Oxford University led by an eminent philosopher. In deference to his eminence we all attended his opening lecture on the first evening. I understood little of that lecture, not entirely because the subject was new to me and the lecturer's treatment advanced, but also because I was preoccupied by the setting of our weekend. The wide sweep of staircase, the panelled walls, the solid, dark-grained dining tables, the lawns in English green, held an atmosphere which came partly from the mellowed blending we see in things and people which have grown together (having been wisely placed together), and partly from the historical and royal associations which the Warden of the Lodge had not allowed us to overlook.

With my natural inclinations cultivated by St Hilary's, I revelled in this atmosphere and in the sense of coming to the place which I had long desired at a distance – the high place of intellectual activity, Oxbridge being the Temple and London a satellite Tabernacle, and the combined presence of Oxford professor, psychologists and fellow-students, a festival that was stimulating and a communion that satisfied.

I do remember one phrase of that lecture, however, for in the discussion that followed it was irreverently taken up by one of our lecturers in psychology, himself a graduate of Cambridge University. With a doggedness made emphatic by a jerk of the unruly mass of his black hair, and with what seemed to me an assumed incomprehension, he asked over and over again: 'But what is "dynamic self-transcendence"?' The professor, broad and upright in build, greying above his wide forehead, a figure of distinction, explained patiently, faintly puzzled at this display of alienation by one who, because of his past advantages at Cambridge, if not his present associations in London, ought to have been at one with his philosophical thinking. But was the psychologist, who often voiced his preference for Anglo-Saxon words, merely challenging the professor to break down his concept into simple language, or did he mean to imply that since such concepts could not be observed and measured they represented nothing?

Nevertheless, the better-known aspects of psychology found their way into the curriculum. A psychiatrist from the Maudsley Hospital gave the third year students a brief course of lectures on abnormal psychology. We were trained to give intelligence tests and practised personality testing on each other, handling a little nervously the lurid shapes of the Rorschach. But this was done in the child psychology department which was symbolically housed at the opposite side of the college from the main section of the department. To the empiricists the link with therapeutic aspects of psychology was a trifle embarrassing. We heard little of Freud and his followers, though one of our lecturers was a psychoanalyst, and another, the focus of our awed interest, was said to have undergone analysis. Professor Eysenck bridged the gap between the behaviourists and the therapists by his diagnostic tests for neurosis based on measurable actions of the patient, and these he expounded to us with dry lucidity.

Thus the leaning towards a pure science prevailed, so that our gentleman from Cambridge was able to deliver this accolade, spoken with well-concealed pride and pleasure: 'Psychology is the most interesting subject in the world but it is quite useless!'

I found when I arrived at university that I had to choose a subsidiary subject. 'Perhaps', I said to the advising tutor, 'I ought to choose something which would be useful at home, possibly a subject which I could teach.' However, my interest was caught by anthropology, which the college offered as the preferred subsidiary to psychology. 'In this college', advised the tutor, 'we believe that people ought to do what they are interested in.' I chose anthropology, and it proved a rewarding choice.

I chose this course because it offered the opportunity to study the races of men. I had waited for this opportunity since that day in the school library ten years before. For special study I chose West Africa because the slaves brought to Jamaica and the West Indies had come from there. My respect for my black ancestors grew as I learnt about their social organization, and with it grew my self-respect. My black ancestor was not a lonely savage, leaping without restraint through the jungle, pleasing himself, attending only to his basic physical needs. Certainly he had few material possessions, but in all other respects he shared the concerns of more technically advanced people – ideas about God and organized religion, patterns of government and social order, and prescribed patterns of behaviour. Moreover, as if to make up for his backwardness in technical development, his system of personal relationships was more complex and in parts more humanitarian than that of more complex societies.

If meeting the gaze of my black ancestor in my imagination had given me freedom, this long close look at him in his own environment was even more liberating. But not entirely. I was still bound up in the question of race and colour. But now I was no longer defenceless and bleeding. My wounds were healing though still sensitive, and I armed myself with the test findings and arguments for racial equality in readiness for battle with anyone who challenged this equality.

England treated us well as overseas students. As a scholarship holder, under the patronage of the Colonial Office, my sister did particularly well: she had tea with the Bishop of London and attended a royal garden party at Buckingham Palace. The Inter-Varsity Fellowship wooed us with intimate tea parties and large international receptions. Other students invited us home during the vacation. We were guests; our visit had a time limit and a specific purpose, and so the English were expansive and welcoming. We did not threaten their castle.

Prejudice, when we met it, was isolated and unusual; I sat one day in a London bus beside a thin, elderly woman who mumbled discontentedly to herself. In the thick traffic the bus idled beside the pavement where an accordion player had his station and the repetitive chords of his music making, which we could not escape, touched off her irritation. She railed at him and then she turned on me: 'Will you get up or shall I?' she snapped. We looked at each other until I came to believe what she meant. I got up, satisfied in the awareness that the people around me were shocked by her rudeness, and a man behind us courteously changed seats with me. Next she caught sight of an un-English-looking man coming into the bus. He was sallow in complexion, he wore a beret and he carried a large canvas under his arm. Her words lashed out again: 'D-n foreigners!'

Like her, the woman on Hampstead Heath seemed abnormal mentally. She was grumbling loudly about the litter of papers on the grass and the children she accused of scattering them, when my sister and I walked up with English friends. Her venom turned on us: 'These d-n Jamaicans', she spat out. 'These bl-dy blacks!' The offence was bearable, even amusing. By what stretch of the imagination were we black? Perhaps it was bearable because of the supporting presence of our English friends. *They* suffered most, it seemed, with acute embarrassment. We started up the conversation again to relieve them.

Rather different was the incident of the clergyman's widow. I was travelling with her nieces and nephews and we stopped for lunch at her large, old house in the country. She was about eighty years old and had lived in India. The colonial air hung about her, about her flat-breasted black frock edged in white lace, the pendant round her neck, the imperious voice. Throughout the meal she addressed me ('spoke' is hardly the word) as 'Miss Jamaica'. (My surname, Nation, was simple enough, but, perhaps because it was English, the English constantly found it difficult to link it with a Jamaican face.)

After the meal, she led me to a window, peered into my face, and enunciated, loudly, 'Now that I see you nearah (pause) you have quite a nice face (pause) and what beautiful teeth you have.' Behind her, her nieces dissolved in suppressed laughter. I was amused myself, for I had been warned of her eccentricity. But I did not laugh for I had other feelings: anger and disgust at being treated like a bird or a reptile, a specimen at the zoo. On another occasion, my sister and I visited the Tower of London. We stared too long and too objectively perhaps at a guard there, so exotically dressed, standing so rigidly at attention. He stuck his tongue out at us. The rebuke was justified. Remembering my own reaction to the scrutiny of the clergyman's widow, I think I know how he felt.

A gentleman, they say, is never rude, unintentionally. The cultivated Englishman is capable of cutting rudeness. He was a senior civil servant and his relatives were mentioned in Burke's Peerage. I sat at table one evening in his flat in south-west London, at his wife's invitation. 'Of course,' he drawled out in his marked Oxford accent, as he dabbed at his mouth with a crisp white table napkin, 'of course, colour is class!' The remark was unprovoked and unnecessary. Was he intentionally rude or no gentleman? Perhaps he thought that as a student I would take up his statement and discuss it objectively. But even so his words showed lack of tact and human sensitivity. The kindest explanation was hardly complimentary to him. Colour is class. The fear put into words and proclaimed as dogma. I had so far evaded the school encyclopaedia's claim that my colour was linked with obsession with sex, and I thought I had disproved the verdict of arrested intelligence. But here was a new limitation, fixing me till death in my place in society. Anguished, I wrestled in heart and mind with the condemnation.

CHAPTER XX

The first vacation loomed up with threatening vacancy. The hall of residence would remain open for part of it, and therefore I had only a short period to plan for. But as I had so little money I needed to find a cheaper way of living. My sister's scholarship allowed her to live comfortably anywhere during the vacation and she had made friends who invited her to their homes from time to time. I could not expect her friends, she reminded me, to take on her sister as well.

The first Christmas worked out in this way: towards the end of the term one of our lecturers appealed for a student to help with her children over the vacation. Two of us volunteered, but the other student generously gave way to me because her home was in London. I had nowhere to go. I was to spend most of the vacation helping in this way but I was to be free over Christmas and a friendly fellow-psychologist invited me to her Hampshire home for that period. I spent my first Christmas there, as well as the succeeding Christmases of my student years. We spent them in traditional English style – a carol service in Salisbury Cathedral, listening to the Queen's speech after dinner when we stood to attention for the National Anthem. It was a quiet, gracious home which had links with British countries overseas and where my needs for warmth and diversion were steadily considered. After that, the vacation problem was settled for the rest of my undergraduate days through my sister who took the problem to the IVF Women's Secretary. She arranged that I spend the long vacation with a large Christian household perennially in need of domestic help and so I was introduced to the warm, boundaried, wholesome life of 'Pa' Salmon's household.

This household spread over three houses on the outskirts of a Surrey village overlooking the South Downs. Pa had built the houses himself. He was in his eighties when I first came to his domain, but in spite of his age, he was its vigorous and effective head. He was a retired clergyman of low churchmanship – so low that one of the more facetious members of his household described him, in hushed secrecy as if he were committing treason, as 'belonging to the basement of the Church of England'. Pa, in his zeal that there should always be men in the church upholding the doctrinal emphases to which he was wedded, took young men into his household and prepared them for entrance to the theological colleges of his choice. He taught their minds and fed and watched their spirits for the life of the Holy Spirit in them and for the love for the Lord Jesus, without which, as he knew, their training and head knowledge would be useless. He guarded their lives – such a wide household needed help (Pa had five sons and daughters and there were sometimes twenty to a meal) and this was supplied by au-pair girls from Europe or students like myself.

Pa's watchfulness and forthright rulings kept us apart, man from maiden, though he could not dampen the exuberance that our mixed companionship produced. We met at prayers, at meals and over the washing-up, when, with the door closed, safe from Pa's eye and ear, we would give way to our bursting spirits in singing, though our songs never strayed beyond the religious theme and the limit of our daring was the syncopated version of the children's chorus: 'There is a joy, joy, joy, joy down in my heart.'

The day was planned and organized for everyone, even for Pa's children who were home from boarding school. 'I go back to school for a rest', said one of his sons. We met for prayers, morning and evening, led by Pa, whose roving eye checked on the presence or absence of every member of the household. 'Where is so and so?' he would ask if one were missing. At these times of prayer I was introduced to the writings of Bishop Ryle, whose certain faith and simplicity and clarity of style seemed to come from Pa himself, for whom Paul's wish to 'depart and be with Christ, for that is far better' was no empty piety, but reflected his own deep longing.

Pa's prayerful concern for every member of his household, new or longstanding, showed itself in endearing words. 'Darling girl' I was when I first came to Pa's house, but later I fell from favour and became 'dear girl'. I cannot help thinking that Pa's judgment of the spiritual state of those under him was in part determined by how far they submitted to himself and all his points of view. Perhaps I fell from favour because at some stage I must have shown detachment from his authority.

'What are you learning in psychology?' he challenged me. 'Naughty things', he answered himself before I could collect my answer, and he offered to pay my expenses if I would leave off my course and go to a women's Bible college he recommended. I was new to the standard of complete submission to God's will and abandonment of everything to His service, and, as I was susceptible to the authority of my elders and betters, I was thrown into confusion by this attack. But I was rescued from my bewilderment and resulting depression by Mrs Salmon, reassuring me to go on quietly with the course I had begun. She shared the central place in that household with Pa, holding all together with her radiance, keeping us secure because she looked to inquire after our need and not to find trivial fault. Her lively Christian joy matched his own deep devotion and her tact and understanding balanced his uncompromising spirit.

In spite of being short of money I also managed to go abroad during my college vacations. Perhaps I missed the abundance of experiences that more opulent students enjoyed, but I did not miss the variety, and the opportunities that came to me, one by one, and seemingly heaven sent, I appreciated all the more keenly.

First I attended a student international conference run by the Quakers, and held that year in the Saar. Someone in authority vouched for my impecunity and I was given grants to cover all my expenses.

The evening before I set off was a turmoil of anxiety: I would surely be seasick on the Channel crossing, and how would I inquire about the trains I must change on my way across France and Germany, for my knowledge of French was useless and my German non-existent? A medical student gave me tablets, and the bursar of College Hall prepared for me tiny tins of biscuits against hunger on the trains. My anxiety was past as soon as I was on my way, and was lost completely in the beauty of the vinegrown hillsides of the Moselle valley.

I arrived in the tiny village of Otzerhausen safely and eventually, though I very nearly lost my way: a fellow-passenger on one train misdirected me about the next train I was to take. When he left the carriage, a girl sitting there scowled at what she interpreted as his wilful misleading and directed me to take a train going in the opposite direction. She proved to be right. I did not waste many thoughts on my narrow escape.

My memories of that conference are varied. It was summer and the conference centre was newly built on the edge of a pine forest. Our nearest neighbours were a farmer and his family. His daughter, Uschi, a warm-hearted twelve-year-old, eager to improve her English, visited the centre and also invited us to her home, where we feasted on strawberry gâteau with fresh farm cream. An indelible memory. The people at the conference, coming from many different countries, made near and real the problems of these countries that before were just small items in newspaper print. There were, among others, the passionate 'Madagash', the embittered German, the two Yugoslav students, one suave, one wild, both earthy and brown-skinned, the exuberant African, and the Arab who amazed me by appropriating to his own people the message of the hymn, 'Jerusalem the Golden'. (Does not Jerusalem belong to the Jews?)

The conference ended with an appeal to us to take up the Quaker way of pacificism. Not all of us could accept this nor the idea of man's inherent innocence and goodness on which it is based, but we all had the experience of sitting in the place of someone else, someone perhaps, who, from our country's standpoint, stood on the opposite side of the political fence – a potential enemy – and the barriers of hostility and ignorance were broken down a little.

A tour of Holland with a party of students and a short holiday in France made up the sum of my excursions abroad, and from these I carry treasures of memory. From Holland there are these: the paintings of Rembrandt in the Rijksmuseum, set in gilt frames, life-sized and deep-toned, with a living, speaking quality that their reproductions lose; the fields of Arnhem with distances of headstones to the English dead, and the still-warm gratitude of the

Dutch for those who died to liberate them. And memories of France: a painter at his easel out of doors by the side of the Seine; the broad walks by the river with the pattern of leaf-shadows on the pavement from the trees bordering it, and the succession of open stalls manned by stolid, darkly-dressed women; the aftermath of a first communion service in the Cathedral of Notre Dame – children coming out onto the steps in the sunshine, the girls in wide white frocks and veils, the small boys in dark, sleek trousers and black bow-ties, and proud parents taking photographs; the splendours of the Palace of Versailles, where the feast of colour and design glutted the mind, and my neck ached as I tried not to miss the intricacies of the paintings that filled the spacious ceilings one after another.

CHAPTER XXI

It was inevitable that my religious self and my intellectual life should come up against each other. Until now I kept my different selves apart. Now the slow and sometimes painful process of integration began. I had to come to terms with biblical criticism. At home in Jamaica I had argued with a friend who asserted that Jesus was not God and I had met students of theology who allowed doubt on the virgin birth, but these had not shaken my own belief. But at university my beliefs were shaken.

In my first year I invited a fellow psychology student to Bible study and she replied, 'But we learnt at school that the Bible is not true; it is a myth.' She was so sure that she was not even going to argue about it. As well I met a general disparagement of Christianity: there was the lecturer, speaking on the way in which theory is built up from experimental findings, who contrasted psychology with theology where, as he put it, 'the superstructure supports the foundations'; there was the professor who, with mild amusement, deprecated Paul's tripartite description of human nature as body, soul and spirit. The first debate of the session victoriously carried the motion, 'This house has no need of God'. It revolved with wit and lightheartedness about the fact that University College was the first college to be established in Britain without a religious foundation. In all these things the message was unmistakable: God is irrelevant. For the first time, I belonged to a community that did not pay even lip-service to God. He was cheerfully dismissed and life was continued efficiently, happily and profitably without regard for Him. The problem centred on the attack of the Bible. If the Bible could not be trusted, how did I know what was the truth?

One day I looked round the collection of Jewish writings in the college library and leafed through a book on the life of Jesus. It was an alternative account to that of the Gospels and I gathered as I read that Jesus was a man and no more, an upstart, an impostor, and this movement a mere episode in the towering annals of Judaism. I did not stop to probe or question. I lacked the confidence to question what I read and to think through a counter-argument. Where did the writer get this information and what basis had I for dismissing it? I put the book down as if it were poison and left the library in miserable confusion. What if all I believed were a lie? The world of Christians shrank in my mind's eye in size and intellectual stature. We were, after all, only a small group in a world of other faiths and unbelievers. Were we clinging to our faith in spite of the facts? Was our faith subjective? I had been dubbed 'religious' by another lecturer. Had I been born in India, he remarked, I would have been a good Hindu. Was that all there was to my faith – a matter of temperament? Was there no choice to be made in terms of the truth between my Christian faith and other religions? Did I believe the Bible only because, by chance, I was brought up to accept it and it was easier to continue clinging to it?

I continued to go the Bible study and there I stumbled on this verse in John's Gospel: 'If any man will do his will, he shall know of the doctrine, whether it be of God ...'. For me at that moment, this was the voice of God. God was saying that the way to intellectual certainty, the way to knowing, began with committal of the will and with obedience to Him. *I* thought that I must suspend decision in my will until I knew for certain with my mind. God said it had to be the other way round. This challenge to my will went deeper than the confusion in my mind and in accepting the challenge I found stability again. But though I saw the real issue to be in my will I knew I could not evade the intellectual search. So I began to read, to listen and to think in order to find the answers to the doubts cast on the Bible's claims. The process still continues.

From what I read I was satisfied that I could trust the books of the Bible as historical documents. My confidence in my fellow-Christians was restored. They were not all evading doubt and clinging to baseless faith. The questions I was asking were already being answered by other Christians able to deal with them, and books were available and talks were given that met my doubts and answered my questions. Was the whole Bible to be dismissed as myth? One reflective glance at the varied types of book that make up the Bible was enough to make nonsense of that claim. But what of the early chapters of Genesis which seemed at that time open to such a description? As I studied physical anthropology and learnt of the progressive changes in Darwin's theory as new evidence was discovered, I realized how important it is to avoid hasty pronouncements where matters of faith and theories of science seem to be in conflict. It was the same for problems of authorship and dating. These I had met at St Hilary's in the context of a believing community and I had not been disturbed by them. Here in the agnostic atmosphere of the university they became weapons to undermine the authorship of the Bible. I began to learn that dealing with these difficulties involved not only research and the use of judgment but also dependence on God, in faith that solutions to these problems did exist even though at the moment I could not find them; that God was able and willing to satisfy intellectual doubts and to vindicate His revelation.

And so it was. As I studied the Bible itself in dependence on God He began to vindicate Himself and His revelation in the Bible. The spiritual unity of the Bible became clear – though the separate books were written over a period of a thousand years or more, yet they present a continuously developing stream of revelation about God and His dealings with men which is consistent within itself and consistent with the continuing experience of Christians since then. The teachings of Scripture became meaningful to me and I proved its claims to be real and powerful in my own life. And this experience I shared with other Christians quite independent of myself. Was this evidence to be discounted? It seems to me to be evidence of the highest order.

But for all this I did not entirely escape the subtle influence of the community I now belonged to – a community where God was irrelevant.

On a mild spring day in the middle of my course, I walked from college to my hall of residence with the sense that everything was just right. My work, the most important thing, was going well and I enjoyed the company of the staff and students. I was secure in this academic world, for me, a blissful world, where outward appearance does not matter too much, where the drudgery of living is the responsibility of someone else, where emotional relationships are in the background and where books and ideas and conversation come first. 'I have everything I want', I thought. 'What do I need God for?'

A few days later I received a letter which shook my world. It served to remind me that there was another world which I had not come to terms with, a world of commitment and involvement, physical and emotional. So far my circumstances had allowed me to escape from this world and where I had come up against it I had not been successful. This letter was from my boyfriend of long standing. He was ending our relationship decisively; he had become engaged to someone else. This break was inevitable because we had drifted apart. We disagreed in particular about my new outlook on religion. However, I had hoped we would agree in time. Now I was being put away for another. I was hurt, even angry. My pride was also hurt. My feelings, I knew, were not praise-worthy, but I brought them to God. 'Let me turn', I thought, 'to Isaiah 53.'

The chapter was very familiar. I had heard it read in church at least once every year throughout my childhood. As it told of Christ's rejection, perhaps I would find it meaningful and helpful now. But the words were cold and dead. Then my eyes fell on the following chapter and there the words came alive.

'Sing, O barren one, who did not bear; break forth into singing … . For the children of the desolate one will be more than the children of her that is married, says the Lord. … Fear not, for you will not be ashamed …; for you will forget the shame of your youth, and the reproach of your widowhood you will remember no more. For your Maker is your husband, the Lord of Hosts is his name; and the Holy One of Israel is your Redeemer, the God of the whole earth he is called. For the Lord has called you like a wife forsaken and grieved in spirit, like a wife of youth when she is cast off, says your God. For a brief moment I forsook you, but with great compassion I will gather you … . For the mountains may depart and the hills be removed, but my steadfast love shall not depart from you, and my

covenant of peace shall not be removed, says the Lord, who has
compassion on you. O afflicted one, storm-tossed, and not comforted, behold, I will set your stones in antimony, and lay your
foundations with sapphires. ... All your sons shall be taught by the
Lord, and great shall be the prosperity of your sons.'

As I read I was not seeing words that had been spoken to the
Jewish people many years before, but I was hearing God speak directly to me. 'Wife', 'widow', 'reproach', 'afflicted', 'storm-tossed'
– my circumstances I knew fell somewhat short of this description. The words did not all apply to me literally. But God was
speaking of more than my present circumstances. He was taking
every hurt, every deep need, every effort to reach out and love, to
understand and be understood, and He was saying, 'I can heal this
hurt; I can meet this need.' He began then a conversation with me
about Himself and about my relationship with other people which
still continues. I had never given Him an opening before. Now He
showed Himself as I had not known nor wanted nor expected Him
to be: close, personal, Friend, even Husband. How had He dared
to use the word? Because He dared I began to see the sexual life
anew. He gave dignity to this side of life; He showed me it was
wholly good, given by Himself. I began to accept myself. I felt
deeply healed. I met God and He did not rebuke nor criticize me;
instead He accepted and lifted me up.

It is impossible to describe what God was like to me in those
moments. I had thought about Him, done duties in His name,
turned my will towards Him and now He captured my feeling, my
emotion. I drew near to Him with my whole being, not just with
part of myself. I was very moved as if everything that ever moved
me deeply were moving me then: meeting after long parting,
magnificent music; as if sunshine and colour, trees, hills and sky
were not still, but alive with joyful shouting; like love at home in
childhood. God was all these things, and more than these things,
and beyond them. The moment passed and I have not been able
to recapture that ecstasy since.

But so much else remained; He put back the enchantment in
life. I was about to put away the love of poetry and beauty in
nature as part of an adolescent phase, unreal and sentimental; I

was about to give way to disillusionment and cynicism. Did music and poetry express independent reality or only some vain fiction of my mind? Could love be altruistic and enduring? Were ideals only another unreal dream? I had been hurt and disappointed often or so it seemed to me. Perhaps my confidence in these intangible things was misplaced and my feeling and desire for them misleading.

But God showed me I was not mistaken in my yearning and expectations: enduring love was not a childish misconception, and beauty and ideals were not an adolescent dream. For He is all these things: He gives them, He embodies them; they have validity in Him. He is love that never disappoints or gives rebuff; He is beauty that does not change or disappoint, security that never lets one down. When I rejoice in these things I rejoice in Him. God is my dream of harmony and perfection come true. Because of the absolute security that I have in Him, I can live with the mixture that I find in myself and in the world around me; I can learn to live with the possibility of sudden disaster and I am able to give love though it may be spurned and cause me pain.

CHAPTER XXII

I fell in love again within a year; in spite of myself, for he was English and I was determined not to marry an Englishman; I included them all in my resentment against the ship's doctor. I had met Graham from time to time since I came up to college; he was a student there and had been president of the Christian Union in my first year. We had interests in common. He too had a personal knowledge of God and of the meaning of the cross, and our tastes and upbringing were alike in many ways.

At his invitation, I had met his parents and sisters, some time earlier, at their home in Kent. Then, as a visitor, an overseas student, I was well received and I felt at home. When I stood a little away from the family as they were gathered for tea in the garden, his mother invited me nearer. 'Come', she said, 'you are in a family now, Joyce.' I was entertained without fuss or strain; no courtesy was overdone. They had the simplicity of life which my parents had taught me to love. The ingredients were the same, though some, being English, were of a different variety: warm affection at home, walks in the afternoon in every weather, gardening in summer, scones and home-made preserves, apples and knitting and a good book by the fire in the evening, and, in addition, a direct and open acknowledgement of God.

But later they firmly resisted our engagement: it would be 'wrong' for their son to have a coloured child, 'wrong' for me to have a white child. This objection came in the first painful moments after Graham had announced in their dining room that there was an understanding between us. I knew the objections to a 'mixed' marriage on social and pseudo-scientific grounds, but a moral objection was utterly new and unexpected. ('All marriages are mixed', an older friend, a barrister, later pointed out to me.) But though they said little at that time, and even tried half-heartedly to show acceptance, I could sense the submerged and surging agony inside them, an irrational, blind pain like that of people in disaster. Our love for each other, Graham's and mine, our unquestioning assumption of our right to marry, had thrust the world of his parents into a storm of dreadful emotion.

I left them to each other and went upstairs, and knelt down to pray, driven to find sanity and reassurance in God from this family that had suddenly withdrawn from me into its own agony caused by me. God had met and comforted me before at a similar time. I would find Him now. But God was silent. In the darkness of my closed eyes I met hardness, a hard, high wall I could not penetrate and that gave back no echo. There was no answer from God. Only solid silence. Yet God was there, silent and unyielding though He was, and I knew His support. I got up from my knees, without relief from the darkness and the hardness of God's restraining 'Wait!'

The battle between Graham and his parents continued for many months. I escaped. I returned to Jamaica. My own parents accepted what I told them without pain or questioning.

I can guess at the reasons for the agony that Graham's parents felt and expressed in their letters to him. I have read enough of the excuses made to justify slavery: that the negro slaves were not fully human but were a kind of advanced ape. Could I forget the passage on the negro read at school? Who would not baulk at the idea of association by marriage with a sub-human species, inferior in intellect, poor in moral discernment and spiritual capacity? And the idea of having grandchildren, marked with this taint, bearing one's name, must be intolerable indeed.

This was not all. Graham's parents are deeply religious, and even the Bible has been used to justify racial apartheid. Had not God 'fixed the bounds of the peoples'? Never mind the verse of Scripture that states that God 'made from one every nation of men'; did not the former quotation mean that there should be no inter-racial marriage? I do not know how many of these ideas lay buried in their hearts, whether they knew them to be there and voiced them, or whether they met them openly from others, but the objections they gradually expressed were cogent enough. They were anxious to save Graham and myself and our children from a world which, however mistakenly, held ideas like this and acted on them. They feared social ostracism for us; they feared for Graham the possible cutting off of his career, and for our children confusion as to their identity. No doubt they feared for themselves the disappointment of cherished hopes centred in their son and the pain and embarrassment over and over again as every relative and friend came to know about it. For do we not assume that things which are painful to us are equally painful to other people?

Yet, in spite of this, on our own, Graham and I knew deep happiness and peace, for in finding each other we had discovered part of our real selves. Life at university satisfied that part of me which was ambitious and sought achievement and recognition. There were definite goals to be worked for, awareness of intellectual growth and the repeated challenge of new people and new places. I was pressing forward from one peak of challenge and achievement to another.

Now Graham was calling out the neglected side of myself. We shared stillness and heard the lark sing. I had neglected this part of myself. It was there but I had given it no room to grow. It took root at Harewood when as small children, my twin sister and I walked in silence with my father, taking his hand. We would stop at a turning in the road where the view was clear and drink in with him the sight of distant hills against the sky and near and farther trees, differing in shape and colour; or we would sit with him in the evening on the darkened verandah looking into the blackness of the thundery night and wait for the flash of sheet lightning that lit up the surrounding scene like a brief moment of eerie daylight. But after Harewood I put this away. Now Graham was calling out this response again and I was surprised and delighted.

I found too that I could share with him my love of books and ideas without fear of rebuke or suspicion that I was seeking to be different or win praise. Sharing like this comes rarely. I would have lost more by refusing Graham than I risked in marrying him. When I returned to Jamaica at the end of my degree course we had made no formal decision. On the one hand it was unnecessary, for we were sure inside ourselves, but while his parents objected so strongly we could not decide. We used this time of waiting as a test: if God wanted us to marry He would make the way clear. If we did marry we would have difficulties and we would risk the problems that his parents raised. But if God allowed us to marry, He could use the difficulties for good, He could meet the needs of our children and indeed this is what we have found.

After three years I was in Harewood again. On my first morning at home I woke up, unbelieving, to freshness and brightness, warmth and quietness. With the physical sensations came too the spirit of earlier years – expectation at the start of a day, security, carefree joy. I got up quickly and dressed. How easy it was to get dressed in few clothes, without fear of the cold outside! I went impulsively and expectantly from the house, down the hill and into a field of coconut and cocoa trees in a narrow valley by a stream overshadowed by well-grown hillside. My hearing, which had been keyed up to the roar of London traffic, that had borne the throb of the engines of the returning ship home, relaxed, and I felt the silence around me that was like a pause in music, rich with the harmony that surrounds it. Around me were my father's trees, my father's land. I was no intruder, I need fear no interruption. The years of striving after achievement abroad, the battle over Graham and the turmoil of pain on leaving England, might never have been. Harewood always brings this, always makes nothing of what happens beyond it and gives renewal and refreshment and the thrust to go forward again. I think that I would be restored from the worst that might happen to me, if I could return home to Harewood afterwards.

I began to do research in education at the University College of the West Indies and this gave me the opportunity to work on material which was dearest to me, material which was peculiarly Jamaican, the dialect and the school situation which I knew so well and which had interested me for so long.

Jamaica was different. The social pattern was changing and this was marked particularly at the college. Here, below the towering heights of the many-breasted Blue Mountains, black face, brown face and white face met and talked on equal footing. They met at leisure on the cool verandahs, in the pleasant gardens of College Common or at work, in the heat of the day, on the college walkways, where the white walls gleamed in the sunshine and the purple flower of the bougainvillea was reflected in the glistening forehead of black face. I was relieved of the burden of the task I had set myself years before in the school library. It was no longer necessary for me to prove by my own efforts that the negro was as capable intellectually as any other race.

There was another significant experience during this time; I had one more severe attack of depression, but this time there was no spiritual crisis. I was living alone in a flat, work was going slowly, my heart was in England and the future was undecided. Cause enough for depression. It was as overwhelming as ever, a nightmarish experience, disfiguring my awareness of the world. But in my spirit I was firm; the battle against God was over. It passed in a few days and I have not had another since. Soon I became engaged, and after eighteen months I returned to England to be married.

CHAPTER XXIII

We were married in London two weeks after I arrived from Jamaica. Graham's parents now gave us their support and three of our four bridesmaids were his sisters. One of our friends sang at the reception. He was a Welshman, and he sang effortlessly like a bird, with a full, rich voice:

> 'If with all your hearts
> Ye truly seek Me,
> Ye shall ever surely find Me.
> Thus saith our God …'

These words had meaning and reality for both of us. Added to our happiness was a deeper joy because we had found Him, and this we shared with many at our wedding. Though none of my relatives could be with me on that day, I belonged to another family and they were with me – a spiritual family that cut across every division of race, class, colour and ability. It was a happy wedding, though it was cold for spring. Those who shared it with us remembered the spirit of happiness and remarked on it afterwards, not out of formal courtesy but with conviction. I was given away by a Jamaican, a friend of my parents who was in London to complete his Bar examinations. Knowing that a wedding in my family in Jamaica would hardly have been complete without wine, he was impressed that on this occasion we served fruit juice only. 'There was no spirit', was his comment, 'but the Christian spirit', and the life it gave brimmed over.

That day I stepped into a new world, utterly new, bewilderingly new, and for which I was ill-prepared. On the one hand it marked the beginning of the fulfilment we had waited for, but for me it also brought a turmoil of adjustment. Without the one, the other would have been unbearable. It was like starting at school and floundering at every task. I had to unlearn some things and learn much for the first time. I am still learning. Most of my time since

I was twelve had been spent away from home. I had become used to institutional life where there were people around me all the time and life was structured by someone else. I was used to putting academic work first. Now I was on my own and often alone; instead of writing essays and unravelling Latin unseens I did the cooking, the washing and the cleaning. I preferred the Latin unseen. Once it was done it remained so. But the tidy room soon became untidy again; the cooked meal was soon eaten and then there was the washing up! Besides I had had more practice at Latin unseens than at cooking and I was better at doing them. I found myself on my knees washing the front steps. It was not a picture of myself I liked at all. At home, the maids always did this sort of job. I was ashamed to find how much it mattered to me to do these menial tasks myself.

Many small hardnesses added up to create my unhappiness in the first years of our marriage. One was the climate. The tropical day receives you with its warmth and brightness, invites you to relax, delights with colour and changing light and gives a sense of well-being. The damp English day is repelling, the cold goads to activity, challenges perhaps, but to the unaccustomed the 'challenge' is painful and cruel, and until you learn not to look, the habitual dullness of a London day clouds and depresses you in spirit. We lived in one rented London flat after another. Only in the evening did the sitting room fire invite to relaxation, but only slowly did it overcome the cold and damp. The warmth built up in front while darting tongues of cold sprang on me from behind. Eventually I would become drowsily comfortable and then it would be bed-time. The bitter bedroom air, the chill touch of the bedclothes would stab me awake until the warmth of my own body sent me to sleep again and tomorrow would bring no escape from the shocks of cold, no relief to body and spirit.

Life in our first flat in Highgate seemed an imprisonment. My small sky was bordered by misted chimney-tops; for pacing-ground I had the solid streets lined with terraced houses, as limiting as prison walls. Sounds of life came through the walls of the cells we shared with the fellow-prisoners and the knowledge that we could also be heard muted our expression of life. We made mock privacy by pretending to ignore our neighbours' lives.

Contact with people was shallow and casual. The milkman said ' 'Ere luv', and marched on; the greengrocer fixed a hard, black eye above my head and said through his teeth, 'Next please!' The butcher rubbed his hands because of the cold and reached for his knife across the saw-dusted floor. The neighbours gave their lives to the god of Routine and ignored their fellow-men under the virtuous excuse of minding their own business. I knew the despair of being a stranger again. Unthinkingly, from habit, I searched the faces that I passed in the street seeking recognition, and the repeated process of giving no greeting and receiving no response produced a death inside. I was part dead in a world of walking dead.

My parents-in-law began to learn to accept our marriage and I to adjust to them. Privately, when we met, we battled with the sense of strain and remembered pain, but gradually, as we spent short periods in their home and joined them in worship, we grew together in acceptance and affection. The moments of embarrassment that we feared did come. On one of our early visits to my parents-in-law, an old friend of the family called after long absence. We stood together with Graham's sisters as Dad identified each one of his now grown family. 'And Joyce, Graham's wife', he ended.

The visitor searched the faces round him in silence, seeking and failing to find the extra one that suited that description. We were paralysed by the dread realized, caught unprepared in an aberrant social moment for which the rules did not prescribe. I brought the moment to an end. I stepped forward and put out my hand to him. After that the dread subsided. Nothing worse of that kind could happen now.

The weekly outing to church should have brought relief from the hardness and drudgery of the week, but it added to my unhappiness. We joined the local meeting of the Brethren Assembly in which my husband had been brought up. Here I found a form of worship quite unlike what I was used to: there was no minister and no written pattern of worship, the varying intervals of silence were broken when someone rose to lead in a hymn, a prayer or a Bible reading. Men only. Women must be silent. Used to an active role in church at Harewood and in school at St Hilary's, I found this ban on my sex oppressive.

When I heard a women's meeting announced I looked forward to it eagerly. But this was not for me. I was twenty years younger than the youngest there and they had come for reasons other than mine – to be soothed and rested, not stirred and challenged to activity, to receive quiet words and thoughts and to pass the afternoon over a cup of tea. Wretchedly I stuck to the Sunday morning meeting, passing the time in watching the fascinating play of broken light reflected from the ruby in my engagement ring. There was no stimulating life, no vigorous challenge to draw me out of myself, no exercising ideas. Only sobering thoughts, often repeated, that set me looking inwards and stirred up the self-pity in my heart. But there was friendliness and frequently an invitation out to lunch and tea.

In the brief eighteen months I had spent in Jamaica working at the University College, I shared the rounded life of the compact community of the college and the older friends outside. This life provided gracious leisure, social gatherings and entertainments with music and dancing, banter and gaiety. At the beginning of our marriage, nothing took the place of these things in my life. We did not find an established community in which these things had a place. Church and university did not provide them and we did not learn till later that we must plan our lives to include leisure and recreation. We did not even own a wireless set and listen to music at home together. The chill drabness I had associated in childhood with Bunyan's writings was now my living experience.

CHAPTER XXIV

Pregnancy came too quickly and made an already bewildering complex of difficulties almost overwhelming. Pride and pleasure – for I longed for a baby – were mixed with the unpleasantness of early nausea. The physical discomforts of progressive pregnancy made me aware of my body as never before. Until now, my body had always obeyed my will. Now I was subject to its limits. My protected and leisured childhood at Harewood, the hedged and ordered life at St Hilary's, were broken only briefly by experiences of physical pain thanks, no doubt, to my hardy ancestors. I knew nothing of physical endurance. A sleepless night because of a tightly-bound finger, infrequent tonsillitis, an epidemic of chicken-pox at school, a few weeks of weakness after dysentery – these were the highlights of my bodily sufferings. Now I was harassed by petty discomforts and by restrictions on my diet and activities.

The London hospital where I was to have my baby brought me a mixture of experiences. I joined the antenatal class where we were well prepared for labour and so enjoyed briefly but regularly the company of others with whom I had something in common: a rich droplet of mercy in those barren days! Here too I gained from the knowledge and skill and conscientious care of the staff, for my baby was saved from a premature birth. But I also knew the indignities and humiliations of being a patient in a teaching hospital: without a 'by your leave', medical students used my exposed body as an object lesson, and I was the subject of a seminar held within my hearing, in which my trouble was referred to as the logical outcome of malnutrition to be expected in someone from an underdeveloped country!

We brought our baby home from hospital in February, coldest February. My arms shook with fearful anxiety at the prospect of going home. How I wished I could stay in hospital, where it was warm, an even warmth with no chill surprises, where, as at boarding school, there was an ordered round, a detailed and unfailing provision for need and where the unemotional sureness of the nurses gave a security that made up for the bare sterile surroundings and the lack of close affection. Home – what did it offer? Home was cold and empty. No bustling, solicitous mother figure had lit a fire or was waiting to welcome me with a meal prepared. And I needed such a person. What had become of the person I thought I was – confident and independent? I had become a child again, dependent, tearful, anxious, needing support and help. I needed my mother as I had not needed her during my years away from her as a student. Those to whom I might have turned were themselves in need of support. I brought with me from hospital the memory of my parents-in-law, their sorrowful, strained faces when they came to visit me in hospital and to see their new grandson. Perhaps the coming of the baby forced on them the reality of our union which still seemed to them unnatural. In time their generous, fair-minded nature prevailed and they accept and love our children warmly, but at first they seemed to feel no joy and I was hurt and disappointed.

Back in our flat my wretchedness intensified. With determined punctuality the baby woke every four hours, night and day, to be fed, and with that deliberate self-absorption that only babies can get away with, he took a leisurely hour to satisfy his hunger. I went straight on from his early morning feed to the task of preparing breakfast, and the prospect of another day, drab, cold and lonely, without hope of rest, in which housework and feeds alternated unremittingly, brought the tears to my eyes.

Cut off from contact with my neighbours, out of my own unhappiness I interpreted their ordinary activities as intentional hostility. If my neighbour shut her bedroom window when the baby cried, I imagined she was expressing exasperation at being disturbed. Perhaps she was. I was never able to make sure. She was at least indifferent. For on the morning after I returned from hospital, I hesitated to go shopping, pushing the pram up the slippery slopes of Highgate's streets. I knocked at her door and asked if she was going out to the shops. 'I am sorry', she said quickly, 'I'm going out to business', and shut the door. I tried my neighbour on

›

the other side who generously offered to keep the baby while I went shopping on my own. I left him with her, grateful but reluctant, as any mother might be to leave her firstborn, barely ten days old, with a virtual stranger.

Later when I ventured out behind the pram I met another woman also with a pram but with two older children as well, their little arms stretched out to hold on to pram or mother, their short legs at a trot to keep up with her steady pace. I was overcome with distress for myself as I watched this group, for they seemed a prophetic symbol of myself. I was no longer free; I was a mother, and the realization did not bring a sense of joyful fulfilment but of unending bondage. I was tied not only to a régime of feeds and pressing tasks but more importunately to a pair of eyes that sought my face as the centre of their being and a life that depended on my caring for its survival, and as long as I lived some vestige of this dependence would remain. I shrank but could not escape from the responsibility for which I felt unfit and which I could pass on to no-one else. I could not see that I would in time accept with joy what seemed a burden then; or even that I could become used to a life that limited and broke up my time and which imposed on me unchosen tasks; let alone that I might find in such a life room to grow, to be myself and to feel free. I could only imagine that the bondage would return and increase itself with each new baby and only death would end it.

Others were sharing my burden, though at the time no sense of relief broke through my numbness and bewilderment. At my mother-in-law's suggestion, my husband began to bring me breakfast in bed to ease the distress of my broken nights. Above all, his pride and excitement over his new son sustained me, as well as his greater knowledge of babies. I was five when my only brother was born; he had three younger sisters when he was old enough to learn to take care of them. He changed nappies, brought up the baby's wind, and confidently calmed him when he cried.

Another strengthening prop was the local health visitor. She found me home help. She herself would stand silent in my kitchen, broad-shouldered, rock-like, competent, pondering no doubt the question she put to the home-help who cheerily passed it on to me: 'She has everything so nice for the baby. Why is she so unhappy?'

My bustling help lived cosily and efficiently in one of those basement flats that offer inviting glimpses of warmth and comfort from the pavement on a cold day. She managed her own flat, her husband and children, and other people's work as well as mine, sustained, she would allege, by snacks of tea and biscuits. One nugget of folklore she passed on to me is with me still, the more memorable for being so absurd: 'They say', she observed one day, 'that the state of your windows shows what your soul is like!'

Now I can chuckle at what might have been a distortion of the quotation about 'eyes being the windows of the soul'. Then I was beyond hilarity. I merely looked at my own windows, untouched except by London grime, and wondered dully at the unfairness that allowed accidents of climate and energy to be the yardstick of one's inner life.

CHAPTER XXV

'What was that about a tortoise?' 'Well, Achilles gives the tortoise a start of ten yards, but Achilles runs ten times as fast as the tortoise, so that one would expect him to outrun the tortoise in a very short time. But we can argue that when Achilles has run the first ten yards, the tortoise is already a yard ahead and when Achilles has run another yard the tortoise is one-tenth of a yard ahead and so on. So it appears possible to prove, contrary to common sense, that Achilles never overtakes the tortoise.' It is breakfast time in our Highgate flat and Graham is unfolding for me the esoterics of mathematical reasoning.

In this way my academic education was continued informally after marriage. Graham introduced me to the world of ideas in which he was immersed, the world of Lewis Carroll and Archimedes, of logic and the history of science, Copernicus and Galileo and the exciting infinities of cosmology. I, in turn, sketched for him the mysteries of Freudian psychology among the other snippets of information I gained at university. Gradually the absorption and seriousness with which we began our exchange gave way to a cheerful tolerance. With defensive superiority I deprecated the uselessness of mathematical abstractions, envious that he could earn his living by an occupation as delightful to him as play, and I heard with regret the disrespectful banter that resulted from his enlightenment in psychology.

I read the papers he prepared for publication and after a gargantuan effort at comprehension I achieved the ability to judge the style and clarity of the language without understanding the matter. I was still close enough to my university days to feel the frustration I knew then as I floundered through the obscure flow of words and misplaced clauses of some academic writing, and with missionary zeal I set out to ensure that my husband at least did not add to the burden of students and increase the pile of non-communicating publications. He took my criticisms seriously and amended his papers with noticeable success, for his readers were delighted that they could understand an exposition of specialist information which was not already familiar to them.

As a result, when the Inter-Varsity Fellowship asked Graham to suggest someone to rewrite for the English market a book which had been translated literally from the Korean, he recommended me. This rewriting took me a long time, three years, for over the same period we produced two more children, crossed the Atlantic twice, settled for short periods in three countries and moved house eight times. But this piece of work gave me the experience and confidence to begin writing as a part-time occupation, and by this ladder I climbed out of my slough of domesticity. For slough of domesticity it was. Even now that I have learnt to cook and enjoy cooking and can take delight in a line of wind-blown washing, I shrink from the domestic image, and all the allurements of the glossy women's magazines cannot dispel the wisps of grey that hang around that image for me.

In Highgate my friendly neighbour who took the baby in while I went shopping was a cheerful, busy mother of two small children. She 'loved' house-work, in all its details, even to the rubbing of the panel work which trapped the dust along every wall of her Victorian house. Happy housewife! (Though her elder child was not so happy – he was often reproved and in tears.) She was content in her life as a housewife, I was not. Yet did I want to be like her? I did try to find satisfaction in the housewife role, but I was soon disappointed. Once in a while I thought I could be moved by the sight of a really dirty floor to scrub and polish until it shone again. Here would be real hard work and the contrast would be rewarding. But at the beginning of marriage my round of duty was neither challenging nor rewarding – I dusted a scarcely dusty room, housework required neither brain nor brawn. And there were too many petty choices to make: shall I shop now or later, spring-clean one room or do the whole flat, spend a leisurely afternoon in central London or stay in and do some sewing? Trivial choices. I longed for people round me instead of unresponsive objects – walls, chairs, a dustpan.

But later when our baby came, my day seemed beset by interruptions and distractions. Nothing could be savoured or enjoyed. Before a task got under way it had to be broken off, a meal had to be prepared, the shopping to be done, the baby to be fed. All had to be done quickly with an eye to the next task. Time became a demon. I thought with envy of my mother's servant, sweating as she scrubbed and polished the wooden floors, rewarded by deep weariness of body and the praise of those she worked for, restful in the knowledge that someone else was preparing her a meal and she could finish her work.

I longed to be out in the world again, the world of people and demanding mental work. When I voiced my longing I was reproved, 'Why can't you make your home and child your career?' I felt guilty – perhaps I lacked humility. Somewhere I thought I fell short of the spirit of a true Christian. I set my face again and again to the task of finding housework fulfilling but I could not deceive myself. Surely it was no fault in me that I was dissatisfied? Did God give ability, training and desire for congenial work only to frustrate them? I was alone in my problem. In my limited world I found no other woman like myself. This was not a man's problem. To be husband and father did not mean an end to every other desired activity. How many Christian men, I thought, trained to be doctors, would adjust contentedly to the role of ambulance drivers? Surely my dissatisfaction was understandable and not blameworthy. Reluctantly I concluded that the reproving voice of my Christian sisters was not the voice of God. They did not understand or share my problem. They spoke from the contentment of their own met needs. I would have to work out my own salvation.

Some years later I found a group of English housewives who shared my problem. One said, 'I am not one of those who find that being a housewife and mother is completely satisfying.' To hear her say this openly, without guilt, and without surprise or shock on the part of her hearers, was balm to my spirit.

But the domestic role brought with it another freedom. In my first pregnancy I spent ten days in hospital under sedation because of a threatened miscarriage. At the end of this time I came very close to another attack of the severe depressions I had known since my school days. This time the moment it began I got up quickly, renewed the sitting room fire and began to prepare the next meal. The threat passed, for I had learnt the way to escape these depressions: this life of doing and serving which I thought I hated was the cure to my illness for it provided balance to my introspective and self-centred self.

My husband bore much in those days. If he ever wanted to escape, to disown even for a little his wife, whose colour brought him problems, he did not show it. Often I would be on the alert when we had to meet new people or his colleagues. Would he evade the introduction? Would he avoid acknowledging that I was his wife? I could not make it easy for him; he did not ask it of me. He stood by me and honoured me. Why should he not? Was I not worthy of his honour and loyalty? But I was still plagued by lack of confidence and self-respect because of my colour. It was a new experience for me to be dependent on another for my sense of value in the eyes of the world. If he disowned me then I was dishonoured; if he was loyal to me, my self-respect remained and his colleagues and his family would also come to accept me. This was in parable a spiritual lesson – I came nearer to understanding my dependence on Christ for my standing before God, and nearer to accepting it. Identified with me, my husband incurred the humiliations of my colour, but he remained true.

This lit up for me the teaching about Christ which I had been hearing and singing about since my childhood: that Christ, though He was God, was identified with me in His humanity, and He took this identification to the extreme limit of 'becoming sin' though He Himself was perfect, and even suffering the punishment of my sin.

We left Highgate for another furnished flat in Hampstead when our baby was six weeks old. Five months later the owners of this flat returned from abroad to claim it. We answered an advertisement for a university couple to live in part of a Georgian house in a London suburb. We were accepted from among twenty applicants. We arrived with our belongings to move in, and our landlady, seeing me for the first time, was thunder-struck. A coloured person, a Jamaican, in her house! She knew the country was being overrun with Jamaican immigrants but she did not imagine the problem would invade her world. She could not help meeting them; they jostled her in the shops and on the Underground. But here in her house she was safe; her home at least was sacred. Now, here was one of *them* within her Georgian house! In her mind's eye no doubt ran livid pictures of depressed areas where immigrant families lived, where the houses were neglected, clothes were dried and humanity spilled over onto the landings and the sound of music was too loud. Never. Not in her house. Not if she could help it. She said little at first, but her face was hard.

The next day she called my husband to her sitting room and berated him for deceiving her by not saying that his wife was coloured. We would have to leave. Her husband was different; he could not check the tide of his wife's anger but he came to the flat and apologized to me.

In a few days my father-in-law came for us and we lived in his house for the next six weeks. I became ill; I was very unhappy and full of self-pity; my hurt feelings raged against that landlady. The incident was swollen up in my mind as part of the 'long history of the white man's inhumanity to the negro'.

I complained to God in so many words: 'Here I was, the wounded representative of the negro race in our struggle to be accounted free and equal with the dominating whites!' And God was amused; my prayer did not ring true with Him. I would try again. And then God said, 'Have you not done the same thing? Remember this one and that one, people whom you have slighted or avoided or treated less considerately than others because they were different superficially, and you were ashamed to be identified with them. Have you not been glad that you are not more coloured than you are? Grateful that you are not black?' My anger and hate against the landlady melted. I was no better than she was, nor worse for that matter. There was no difference. As far as God was concerned we were equally guilty, and guilty of the same wrong. We were both children of our background, caught in the deceitfulness of false values and emphases. I could not preen myself and say, 'Here is one sin I will never be guilty of. I am the victim,' for while I was victim for one moment, the next I was myself the offender. We were both guilty of the sin of self-regard, the pride and the exclusiveness by which we cut some people off from ourselves. And this is common to all men.

We lived next in Edgware, near London, and there we were happier than in any other place before. We found a friendly church and good neighbours. Our flat was above a butcher's shop – a kosher butcher. I would buy from him small cuts of meat for my small family as we needed it, while his richer Jewish patrons bought large stocks to last for days at a time and their bills ran into many pounds. After six months we prepared to leave for Jamaica where my husband was to lecture at the University College. I said goodbye to our butcher and he surprised me by the warmth of his reaction: 'It is not the money that you have', he said, 'but it is the spirit that is in you.' Thank God. In spite of the unhappiness and the buffetings, I was still myself, still whole, still carrying on, still able to meet the people and the demands of the world around me, and that wholeness and that spirit came from Him.

CHAPTER XXVI

Our two years in Jamaica healed and restored me in many ways. In Edgware although we were happier, I had been unwell. I was worn out by the cold and months of insufficient sleep. Daily I struggled in the situation commonplace enough to the young English housewife, but alien to my experience, where a mother copes singlehanded with both baby and household duties. I found myself at the launderette supporting him on my hip with one hand while I pulled the clothes out with the other, or bearing with his screams and the disapproval of the other customers if I left him in his pram, and I wished there was another pair of hands to help with one duty while I coped with another. Tried by these things and constantly on the alert, I grew thin, an early intestinal trouble recurred and I had repeated attacks of tonsillitis.

At home again in Jamaica, I wondered if I would ever feel like my former self again; confident, with a sense of well-being, pleased with the activities of day-to-day living and able to take a sustained interest in them.

I lay in bed in my sister's house and relaxed completely for the first time in many months, knowing that my baby was safe with someone else and that I need not be disturbed. As I lay on the old-fashioned four-poster bed in that high, cool room, polished, well cared for, and comfortable with age, the sounds that came to me from the household below merged evenly with the brooding quietness, and through the windows came the light of the sun-filled sky against which were figured the gaunt lines of a giant fig tree. My burden of continuous responsibility and vigilance was lifted for a little. More than this, I was not causing undue strain to anyone else for my sister had household help.

My sister's house had been built over a century before by the second generation of an English family who came to Jamaica as Methodist missionaries to the slaves. Solidly built of stone, with walls nearly two feet thick on the ground floor, it had withstood the battering of recurrent hurricanes and earth tremors over its 100 years. It appears undistinguished from the outside except for its sweep of double staircase and long verandah enclosed with carved woodwork, but it stands 2,000 feet above the sea on the crest of a hill, commanding a wide view, from the back, of jagged rock and overgrown hillocks and, from the front, of more open country bounded by the inescapable distant hills – a bare landscape by Jamaican standards, that is from time to time redeemed by the colours of the sunset over its western horizon. But though bare to our eyes which had feasted on the profusion of Harewood's scenery, to the family from temperate Britain who had built and lived in this house, this landscape, matched with mild sunshine and the turquoise blue of the sea-reflecting sky, must have given reality to a dream of eternal summer in the Yorkshire dales or Scottish countryside.

To welcome our arrival a special meal was prepared, remarkable for its variety of dishes: there were yams and breadfruit, potatoes, pears and pumpkin, and leafy salad vegetables of different kinds. We counted nearly a score of different foods. The 'feast' was served by the male cook, transformed into butler for the occasion by a white coat, cream flannel trousers and a black bow-tie. But his manner was not transformed and his strained, wary look and quick plunging movements seemed better suited to the out-of-doors and to more dangerous pursuits than waiting on subdued and travel-weary guests in that secure, time-dignified dining room.

We travelled round the island meeting my relatives in a tiny black Austin, straight-backed and British, that had belonged to Graham's father. Having come all the way from England with us by boat, it was now subject to the indignities of Jamaican travel: it stalled on the steep hills, jerked up and down over the bumpy roads like a bowler-hatted English gentleman being jolted ignominiously on his seat by some mischievous urchin beneath it.

We visited my grandmother, daughter of the pair in the high Edwardian collar and riding habit respectively, whose portrait was passed round the family. Though she was past eighty she was still active, read voluminously and sewed, and her glossy black hair lying close round her head was not noticeably greying. In her teenage years she used to ride with some of her sisters (she had fifteen brothers and sisters) in a horse-drawn carriage where there was hardly room for the hooped skirts they wore, and even now she still wore the stockings, the calf-length dresses and the eight petticoats of those earlier days. Her husband had died while three of her nine children were still at school and her youngest daughter of typhoid at the age of twelve. A book given to her by a clergyman to comfort her at that time – a copy of Rutherford's *The Loveliness of Christ* – she kept for many years and then passed on to me. Her bearing and her spirit were marked by the hardship and severity of those days but her children have rewarded her by sustained devotion and support. After they were grown up, three of her five sons would come every morning to her cottage for coffee. One lived with her, the other two were married and lived nearby.

From time to time the others came, my father and another son who lived in Kingston, bringing their families with them. This was a special outing. We would pile into three cars for the long journey and eventually arrive in Granny's yard, shouting and cheering. Granny would come down the path and stand between the naseberry tree and the log-covered water tank and reprove us sharply: 'Stop the noise inna me yard!' But a scant tear would moisten her eyes and a wide smile force its way across the stern, thin-lipped face as her children and grandchildren, scarcely abashed, tumbled out towards her. When Graham and I brought little Graham, our son, her great-grandchild, to see her, she said, 'I never thought I would see this one!'

Little had changed since my childhood. Her rocking chair stood on the bare, polished floor of the sitting room, the walls of which were lined with photographs of the family and among them a large coloured picture of the Queen and the Duke of Edinburgh. A sewing machine and a four-poster bed covered with a patchwork quilt still all but filled the bedroom where, as a small child, I would vie with my cousins for the privilege of sleeping with Granny. In the dining room we ate crisp, flat 'bammy-bread' and fried fish, and sugarcane cut from the small patch growing near the house.

This is the savannah-land of St Elizabeth where the cassava and corn grow and in the rocky hillsides goats are kept. Life comes hardly out of this red clayey soil for the rainfall is uncertain and the sun beats unmercifully. Since our visit bauxite has been found in these parts and the bulldozers that for some time threatened Granny have finally driven her from her long-held homestead. Now at ninety-two she sits in Harewood, still alert, only less active, more softened by the kinder, lush, varied country round my father's home, still reading voluminously, sewing and, in keeping with the times, watching the television.

In our first year in Jamaica we had another son, again at a teaching hospital attached to the University College where my husband was lecturing. This time there was a ruling that the medical students did not examine wives of the members of staff and when this was done by mistake I received a careful apology. Bit by bit my self-respect was being restored.

The contrast between my experience of childbirth in London and Jamaica could hardly have been greater. Graham Junior was born on a dark winter evening and in the enclosed labour room, lit artificially; the masked figures of the medical students and nurses moved like a throng of shadows. I worked hard in that room for what seemed hours. A midwife stood, poised like a trooper, on either side of me, and one shouted 'Push!' at intervals, as if she were conducting a gym class.

In Jamaica, Geoffrey was born in early afternoon. Sunshine flooded the room from the windows that stretched its length, facing south-west. One doctor and one nurse were with me and they occupied themselves at one end of the table with a coolness of detachment that was almost indifference. There was a test-match in progress somewhere in the world that day, and occasionally a head popped round the door, above a white gown, and informed my companions of the latest score! It was a casual, leisurely affair, and when it was over I was left with a lively, dark-eyed baby, wondering that it had happened so quickly.

Later, from my room in the maternity wing of the hospital, I looked out through French windows at the green lawns and the orange and purple bougainvillea in bloom. Some of those who worked there and who came to visit me I had known since childhood. At home, my mother and a competent maid took care of the family, and when I returned home, a basket of splendid blooms added to my welcome. There were strains and difficulties with this new baby as with the first, but these were not uppermost and there was help at hand. When Graham Junior, then two years old, expressed his jealousy by making havoc at the baby's bath-time, a neighbour, English but at leisure, came regularly at that time to distract his attention. My great-aunt lived nearby with her daughter, a nurse, whose help and advice were a great source of strength in the baby's early months.

We lived first on a new housing estate – row after row of slab-concrete bungalows painted in pastel shades, each set in its own garden, well kept or otherwise. Through the open doors and windows from next door we heard the voices of happy children at play or chanting their homework, but we saw little of them. A snapshot records one of their infrequent visits. It shows Graham Junior scrambling over the garden wall, his mass of white curly hair standing out in contrast to the cluster of black faces surrounding him with amiable curiosity.

We moved after a year and went to live on the college campus in a house belonging to another lecturer who was away with his family. Over against the restraint of living with other people's furnishings was the advantage of being more comfortable in a large house, well planned, convenient. Honeysuckle crowded over the east windows and shaded the sitting room from the morning sun, and the large garden was kept by someone else. We were here when the fierce Hurricane Flora of 1961 threatened to hit Jamaica directly. I prepared to boil drinking water and to do the cooking on a small paraffin stove, to feed the family out of tins and to keep the belongings of the absent householder safe from damage, but the threat passed. Our escape, however, meant disaster for others. The hurricane veered off its course while it was only a few hundred miles away from

Jamaica and headed for the mainland, crippling British Honduras instead.

Among the restoring features of these two years – warm sunshine, household help, the nearness, once again, of close relatives and long-known friends – was the opportunity for congenial work. On one of my visits to the University Health Centre I was seen by the doctor in charge who also directed the Department of Preventive Medicine. He asked me what subjects I had read at university, and when I replied, 'Psychology and anthropology', he exclaimed, 'You are just the person we want to lecture to the medical students on the social background of Jamaica!' There were other openings as well. Once again I was doing what I enjoyed, and I was needed for these things. My training and interests were not useless, unnecessary extras, which as a housewife I was better off without. Moreover I could also fill the housewife's role, for home ran smoothly with domestic help and the new baby was happy and manageable.

I took the opportunity of this favoured time to have my tonsils removed while my sister took care of my family. I recovered quickly after the first waking to pain and the choking flow of blood. One of the medical students to whom I had lectured came to visit me, his genuine concern overriding his tact, for he inquired earnestly whether the surgeon had by mistake removed my soft palate in the operation. I had been ignorant of this possibility, but I squashed the first twinges of alarm and restrained myself from hasting to look, reminding myself that the anxieties of a little knowledge were often unwarranted anyway, and so I relapsed into the comfort of my initial ignorance. I was quite justified in being comfortable. Soon I was well again and I have had no further trouble of this kind.

CHAPTER XXVII

It was May 1962 and we were soon to return to England. We were to go by way of America where Graham was to spend three months working at the Massachusetts Institute of Technology. I had never been to America, though friends and members of my family lived and studied there. The prospect brought anxieties. It was trying enough to leave home again to return to the place of hardness from which I had escaped for a while; now, we were going out with two small children, one still a baby. How would the baby be fed on the plane, for he still had a bottle? Would our temporary home be suitable for the children? I feared more humiliating experiences because of discrimination, for already we had been advised to live on one side of the river in Boston rather than the other because I was Jamaican!

I knelt down in my bedroom one morning, while the nappies dried in the hot sun, the baby slept and Graham Junior was at a play-group, and I poured out my trouble to God. Once again He was near in compassion and generous in His promises. I read, again from Isaiah:

'For you shall go out in joy, and be led forth in peace; the mountains and the hills before you shall break forth into singing, and all the trees of the field shall clap their hands.'

God kept this promise in detail, though I could hardly have imagined then how the poetry of singing hills and fields with clapping hands would be transformed into reality. The plane journey went smoothly; before I asked, the stewardess brought a bottle with milk at the right temperature for the baby. At the airport we were met by my cousins and my mother who had arrived some weeks before. But the whole journey lasted twice as long as we expected: the hours we gained in flying were lost again, circling over New York while we waited for a landing strip to become vacant, ambling through customs, making a new plane booking for

Boston because we had missed our connection. But the children accepted all without fretfulness: the noise and the frequent changes of surroundings, the thronging crowds and traffic. They played on the ramps in the customs hall and fell asleep on the second plane journey. This proved a mixed blessing, for on our arrival at the Boston airport we had to carry both luggage and children. I came to a swing door, a sleeping child over one shoulder, and carrying a suitcase in the other hand. A woman passed through the door ahead of me and let it swing back in my face. My husband also had both arms occupied and he was pushing another case before him with his foot, but people stood or passed us by, indifferent. The signs were unmistakable: we were once more among the over-civilized.

It was late evening when we landed in Boston and we missed the friend who came to meet us. We spent the rest of that night being driven up and down the streets in a taxi trying to find our house, until at two o'clock in the morning we realized that the houses were numbered in fours! But the children remained asleep.

The house to which we came belonged to a large family who were abroad. It stood on a wide, pleasant, tree-lined street and was stocked with every aid to pleasure and convenience that the affluent society could afford: gadgets in the kitchen, toys for the children, books, games, records, a television set. Our three months there were an enchanted time. We met no unpleasant experiences because of my colour; rather, perhaps, the reverse. Our first visitors, who came to welcome us the day after we arrived and who later entertained us in their home, were a white American couple. The husband was attached to the Institute where Graham was to do research, but they were also active workers in America's National Association for the Advancement of Coloured People. I could not help wondering whether it was the fact that I was coloured that prompted, at least in part, their kindness to us.

Graham worked before lunch and in the afternoons took us by car across the Mystic River Bridge and over the sweeping highways to the beach. My mother spent six weeks with us and sometimes in the evening she set Graham and myself free to go out on our own. We would wander by the river where every summer, at the bequest of a public benefactor, a Boston orchestra played for the public, free of charge, and we listened in the idyllic setting of broad river, soft, low grass, flowers, coolness and half-light, with hundreds of other quiet listeners there.

In church on Sunday I met again a favourite mistress from my schooldays at St Hilary's. She was doing research in botany and she introduced us to the Arnold Arboretum where she worked: acres of trees and shrubs, each deliberately planted, but casually placed or arranged for pleasure in a maze. There we roamed and picnicked and played, away from the crowds and the roar of traffic.

The last few days before we sailed for England we spent in New York with friends and relatives – another hectic time of change and sight-seeing and improvised living. We sailed in the Queen Mary, proving, by comparison with our outward voyage to Jamaica, that it is far better to travel as second class to the freight in a small banana boat than as tourists in a luxury liner. Always a poor sailor, I found that my best minutes on board were those I spent each day in a bath of hot salt water.

We were returning to England, I restored in health and stronger in spirit, and both wiser about the practical details that would make our life happier. Chief among these was this: we would buy our own house and it would be warm!

We disembarked at Southampton in September 1962. The rain fell steadily down, and the skirt of my woollen suit, which I had last worn two years before, was three inches too long!

CHAPTER XXVIII

'*Why* have I come back to England?' For six weeks after our return we lived with my long-suffering parents-in-law. Graham had given up his post in London and was to lecture at Southampton University. While he went house-hunting I waited in Kent with the children. I waited with some hope that the dark London days would not be repeated, but the future at best had no form and was inevitably streaked with grey from the past. This, the chill damp weather to which we had returned and the hours limited to the needs and company of the children moved me to ask myself, 'Why have I come back?' Had I been free to please myself, to secure my own comfort and happiness I would certainly not have returned.

We found our first home in time; it was a bungalow eight miles outside Southampton, in strawberry-growing country and near the yachts on the river Hamble. Through the front windows we looked out on tall trees and from the kitchen window I could see the garden and the sky. Graham Junior, now three years old, having known only the constraints of living in other people's homes, jumped in freedom on his bed saying, 'This is my bed!' He kept asking, 'Whose garden is this? Whose chair is this?' as if to experience again and again the pleasure of hearing, 'This is yours – this belongs to all of us!'

Because of our past experience we now thought carefully about the church we would attend. It was not enough that we find the nearest church of the denomination in which we were brought up. I was insistent that my one regular outing in a week caught up in a narrow round of drudgery should provide wider vision, stimulating thoughts and refreshing and enlivening fellowship. We chose to go into Southampton to the Above Bar Church, whose minister we had known in our student days when he sometimes addressed our Christian Union. Here my needs were answered.

Soon after we began to attend this church, the minister, Mr Leith Samuel, announced a Young Wives' meeting at his

home, and I went to it eagerly. He was standing at the door to welcome those who came, and he exclaimed as he shook my hand,
'How nice to see you!' as if he had met me before. Pleased as I was
with his greeting, I could not account for this recognition. I remembered him easily, standing out before us as the speaker at our
student meetings, but to him surely I was just one face in a
crowded hall of listeners. Then he continued, 'Faith Nation,
twelve years ago!' and I understood. He was taking me for my twin
sister, whom, as an overseas student, he and his wife had entertained in their flat in London so many years before. I warmed myself in the glow of their welcome, mistakenly though it was
applied, amazed at the feat of memory of my host, and grateful for
an identical twin who stirred so warm a memory after twelve years
to ease the strangeness of my entry into a new group.

At the university I was also quickly made to feel at ease, encouraged by the sociable professor of Graham's department, a
Welshman, who readily included us in the sequence of his lively
gatherings.

But elsewhere I felt uneasy and I was on my guard for signs of
prejudice against me, particularly when I met people or entered
places for the first time, in a restaurant, perhaps, or a doctor's waiting room. Would some excuse be made to turn me away? As I
walked by the new housing estate near our bungalow, with its neat
lawns, freshly painted doors and window frames, and luxuriously
draped curtains, I wondered, would my presence be resented?
How deeply felt and how widespread was the objection to my
colour? The questions came with every new encounter. I might
meet rejection anywhere from anyone. I could not be sure that I
would be accepted until I proved it, and over and over again I had
to fight against the desire to hide myself and evade the proving encounter in order to escape the possible pain. In turn I rejected the
world around me, even the trees and the neutral things of nature.
I said, 'These are not mine as are the mountains and the sunshine
of my own country', and their beauty brought me pain and homesickness. But was this not God's world, my Father's world? Why
did I allow the imagined hostility of others to rob me of the power
to rejoice and take my place in it?

Gradually the medicine of acceptance, as I received it repeatedly, changed my poisoned outlook. In my new neighbourhood some accepted me at our first meeting. My new doctor reassured me from the start by his compassion and courtesy. I was reminded of the time when I was ill in my parents-in-law's house after we had been thrust out of the flat in Chigwell. The doctor who came to see me, knowing that I was unhappy and the reason for it, had said, 'Remember that wherever you go people will accept you for what you are and not for what you look like.' Time eventually turned this statement, which then I could only long to believe, into a reality of experience.

Mr Samuel asked me to call on another member of the church who lived near to us and I went with misgivings, prejudging her reaction as she opened the door on a brown-faced mother with two small children. But she received me like an expected guest. After that she often came to see me and sat in my kitchen over a cup of coffee. We came to an arrangement over churchgoing that suited us both: she kept the baby while I was at church in the morning and in return Graham took her family into the evening service.

After a few months another neighbour called. 'I have often seen you at the bus stop on Sunday going into church', she said. 'Would you like to join us in a Bible study group?' And in this way we were joined to a local fellowship of Christians.

Slowly, as I went about the local shops and streets, and people smiled at me in recognition, I began to forget that I looked different from my neighbours and I lost the fear of being rejected.

CHAPTER XXIX

There was sunshine that first autumn in our bungalow. The washing danced in the wind and the children played safely in the enclosed garden where I could see them from the kitchen. I decided that there was room for another baby. With the first waves of nausea came also the snow of the hard winter of 1962–63. As we had resolved, our house was centrally heated and in my lowest moments I hid my tears in the airing cupboard, clinging to the boiler for greater warmth.

The memory of that period is often reinforced because it was then that I first heard the children's afternoon programme on the BBC, 'Listen with Mother'. The opening music of that programme still takes me to the small room in which I sat with the children after lunch. For six weeks, day after day, I looked out dismally on the crisp, white blankness that before was green and brown, until 'a quarter to two' when for fifteen minutes I lost my wretchedness in the protecting maleness of George Dixon's baritone rendering the 'Grand Old Duke of York' or 'catching fish alive' and in the crisp, feminine sweetness of Julia Lang's account of the adventures of small children, greedy pigs and ducks that conversed like people.

After the winter, life became easier and more pleasant. I found someone to help me in the house and I was learning more of the art of being an English housewife. We began to make friends whom we invited to our home and who entertained us in return. With this improvement in my circumstances, my besetting temptation to have my own way returned. I wanted to get on with life as I chose; I did not want God to tell me what to prepare for a meal or to cry 'stop' when my mind raced ahead with plans for the day. I was tempted to congratulate myself for the difficulties overcome in the past and for the present sense of inner confidence and security.

Our third son, Malcolm, was born in a Hampshire nursing home which was originally a stately home, built by Lord Nelson for Lady Hamilton. My sister-in-law, then only seventeen, took charge of the family, mothering the children (who loved her) and managing the household efficiently. For five blissful days in the nursing home I rested and wrote and gazed out on the green of lawns and shrubs in the early, mild September, finding the parade of staff and patients more entertaining than the television which rudely disturbed every afternoon.

An Irish staff nurse, herself a grandmother, would bounce up and down in the aisle touching her toes, more for the purpose of demonstrating her own spry fitness than for instructing us in post-natal exercises. She lingered at the end of her rounds to regale us with personal stories and a rhyme about Arabella Miller and a hairy caterpillar which incongruously produced much mirth, for it was not remotely funny; but the telling of it was good and the situation and the audience well chosen. The night sister plumped my pillows, remarking dryly, 'Well dearie, you look a right mess but I suppose you feel comfortable', which pleased me immensely until I heard her repeat it on another evening to another patient. But I was no longer the child who resented the weaknesses of others and felt keenly her own self-importance, and these things did not spoil my enjoyment nor my appreciation of those around me.

Three months later, on a Sunday afternoon I stood at my front door waving to Graham and the older children as they set off for a walk. I was staying behind with the baby to rest. At that moment a boy went by on a bicycle and shouted at me, 'Nigger!' Quickly I glanced at Graham and the children, hoping they had not heard him, and then I turned indoors, my heart and mind in turmoil. A poisoned arrow had found its mark, a ghost from the past had visited me, and I was unprepared and vulnerable. The picture I had built up of an accepting community vanished. Once again I lived in an insecure world where thorns were waiting to wound in unexpected places. Where was the mastery of myself I thought I had gained – the freedom from concern about colour and race? I was hurt and I was angry and I had to find expression for my raging feelings. Aggressively, I came to God with more boldness than I had ever done before.

I would teach that boy! I would show him that I was not to be belittled!

'Lord, let me reprove him!' Silence.

'Lord, let me speak to him firmly and kindly to show him that I am above being made angry by his taunt.'

'Lord, let me teach him that he is mistaken in his attitude to coloured people.'

God remained silent at each suggestion. He had no more to say to me about race and colour. He had said enough.

My own heart said, 'In all these things you only seek revenge.'

Then unaccountably I was at peace. I got up from my knees but continued listening. I *used* to think that when I was distressed, this was God's punishment or condemnation. I did not think so now, but I still asked the question, 'Lord what are you saying in this?' and the rejoinder came, 'Will you trust *Me* more, walk with Me step by step?'

In that moment, as with the poet, Francis Thompson, the footsteps of my Pursuer halted by me, but from the hand that overshadowed me came, not Love's caress, but the firm grasp of the Master, compelling and mastering without enslavement. I knew that I was still free to turn away from Him and this freedom made me afraid. How awesome that I in my weakness had power to say 'No' to God whose strength I needed, and how I grieved to consider that I was free to turn from God's way and so lose the way to freedom!

The searching questions came thrusting with blades of cutting keenness:

'Will you give to Me the plans you lay when each day starts, and leave the day to Me to order as I choose?

Will you do for Me, the uncongenial task, the drudgery?

Will you bear for Me the trying moments, fretful children, interruptions?

Will you bring to Me each disappointment, the praise of others, love turned unkind, the hindrances to freedom and the frustration of desire, fear, weakness, gladness, guilt, all to Me?'

So God pressed home His claims on me, and so He showed Himself to be not only love giving Himself for me even to death, but also jealous God making demands on me. In this I saw that He was shadowed as truly in the probing insistence of Miss Hobbs as in the supporting nearness of Miss Ealing. In childhood I had felt the claim of God as a nightmare which I could not face and yet I did not want to evade it altogether. In adolescence I had turned away from His claim completely, fearing to lose too much. Now I was more prepared to yield – He had prepared me.

The trees that I watch from the windows of my bungalow are thick with green leaves in summer, and in the autumn I see them turn riotously to mellow tones of russet, brown and gold, then fall away. In winter the thin limbs stretch starkly in the cold, grey sky, jerking ungracefully in the wind, like very old people bearing sorrow without softness. But in the spring I never fail to be surprised that the green buds start from the dark, bare wood, folded, delicate, brushed with soft down, and later burst into glorious, full-dress green again.

I am like these trees, but while *they* part with all of last year's leaves, I still cling to some of the spent fruit and dying leaves of the past like the dread and dreams of childhood, the fears and ambitions of adolescence. I feel their going painfully and how hardly I take my winters!

Yet as surely as with the trees before my windows, the new buds burst, unlikely, unexpected, and are followed by the fullness of summer.

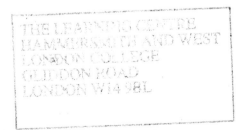